Other Titles by Silvie Graf:

Montana Quest

The Gift

The Final Kiss

Available in E-book format from www.amazon.co.uk and www.amazon.com

Copyright © by Silvie Graf

All rights reserved. Without limiting the rights under copyright reserved above, no part of this publication may be reproduced, stored or introduced into a retrieval system, or transmitted in any form, or by any means 5electronic, mechanical, photocopying, recording or otherwise) without the prior written permission of the copyright owner of this book. This novel is a work of fiction. Names, characters, places, brands, media and incidents are used fictitiously. This book is licensed for your personal use only. This book may not be re-sold or given away to other people. Thank you for respecting the author's work.

Prologue

Steven Hefner stood in front of the bathroom mirror, smiling at his own reflection. From the stylish cut of his dark hair to the crisp white shirt and conservative red tie, his appearance was exactly as it should be for a would-be senator. He knew that with his winning smile, charming demeanour and suave sophistication, the race for the post to become the next senator was only a formality. He'd been schmoozing with the most influential people for some years, making sure he was known to those who could smooth his way into power, donating to the correct charities and being seen in the right circles. He'd worked hard at promoting himself and what he stood for and now, it would soon come to fruition. Once the campaign was over, he would be the new senator. With a satisfied grin, he turned and left the bathroom. His good mood was somewhat diminished as he cast a glance at the girl on the bed. She lay there motionless, the sheets tangled to one side, her naked body showing the signs of his activities throughout the previous night. He studied her for a moment, taking in the marks he'd left on her soft white skin, the sight of the blood smearing her thighs and her breasts sending a thrill through his system as he remembered the events that had put them there. Dammit, but she'd fought like a tiger and if that wasn't a turn on, he didn't know what was. He'd enjoyed breaking her, after all, he'd waited months for this and she had certainly been worthy of his patience. Under the guise of wanting to discuss her future, he'd asked her to come to his study. After all, she was his stepdaughter, and following the recent death of her mother, his responsibility. Enduring yet another silent dinner, the girl was such a sullen, spoilt little bitch, he'd given her a small glass of wine, saying that at sixteen, she was now old enough to have a drink. He had watched as she took a careful sip, a small grimace on her face. Of course, he'd encouraged her to finish it, after all, a silly teenager wouldn't know what a fine red wine should taste like and anyway, the small amount of roofie he'd poured into the glass beforehand was tasteless. He'd been careful not to put too much in, he didn't want her unconscious for what he had planned. No, just enough to make her pliable but awake enough for her to know who was in charge. He didn't need to wait long for the drug to take effect and she was docile enough as he led her upstairs to her bedroom. Getting her to strip for him had been the easy part, he'd noticed that despite the drug, she'd been reluctant but had done his bidding anyway. It was after, as he played with her, that she came out of her stupor and that's when he'd had the most fun, marking her with his teeth, subduing her with his cock and making good use of every available orifice her slender body had to offer. Her tears and cries of pain had only heightened his pleasure and he'd enjoyed the hours spent with her immensely. At some point she'd passed out and even now, as he stood staring down at her, her breathing was shallow, the small movement of her breasts rising and falling the only indicator that she was still alive. Her long blonde hair was a tangled mess, several clumps of it strewn across the bed and on the floor where he'd pulled it so hard, it had come away in his hands. Pity he had to leave for a few days, the campaign to make him senator was gathering pace. Still, she'd be here when he came back and he would have her again. With a satisfied smile on his face, he turned away from the bed and left the room.

***

Frozen from fear and pain, the girl on the bed didn't move for a long time, too frightened in case he came back. She lay there, drifting in and out of consciousness, and when she finally woke up, she found the room in semi darkness. With a horse moan, she pulled her legs up, curling her arms around her knees, breathing hard to try and calm the terror within her. She had no idea how long she sat there but as her breathing slowly returned to a normal level, she gingerly unfurled her body, groaning at the pain shooting through her every limb. It seemed to take forever but she managed to get her legs off the bed and tried to stand up. A sudden wave of dizziness threatened to knock her back, her head spinning and her stomach recoiling at the movement. With gritted teeth, she tried again and this time, she succeeded. With slow, heavy steps, she made it into the adjoining bathroom, clinging to the counter of the bathroom cabinet and then slowly lifted her head. The face staring back at her from the bathroom mirror was one she didn't recognise. Struck dumb with horror, she took in the swollen eyes, the left one almost completely shut, her cracked lips covered with dried blood. And then she saw the bite marks on the side of her neck. Clear imprints of teeth that had punctured the tender skin, droplets of blood had dried at the base of her neck and on her shoulder. Incomprehension flooded her system, all she could do was stare. Shuffling closer, she saw bite marks on her breasts and more blood, forming an ugly pattern where it had dried against her too white skin. Somewhere in her brain she screamed but no sound came out of her devasted mouth. Stunned, she turned away from the image and shuffled over to the shower, turning it on. Stepping under the hot water, she flinched as the jets hit her wounds but she stood still, unwittingly knowing that the water would at least get rid of the blood. Carefully, she got hold of the soap and started washing her bruised and aching body. How long she stood there, she would never be able to recall later. Instinct was starting to kick in, the need to hurry and get out almost overwhelming her. Trying to stem the tide of panic threatening to render her immobile, she hurried to rinse her hair and then switched the water off. Drying herself and getting dressed took most of what little strength she had. Only the knowledge that if she didn't get away as soon as possible kept her from curling up into a ball and let fate take its course. Patting herself dry, she dropped the towel on the floor and made her way back into her bedroom. The sight of her bed with its crumbled sheets, stained with her blood brought another surge of panic. Fighting to keep control, she stood motionless, waiting for the panic to subside. Forcing herself to take deep breaths, she walked over to her wardrobe. Hurriedly, she grabbed a bag from her closet and started to pack as many of her clothes as she could fit along with toiletries and shoes. She zipped up the bag and without a backward glance, she left the room, pausing in the hallway. The house was quiet, too quiet really. Normally there would be sounds coming from the kitchen or from one of the many rooms as staff were busy doing their work. She wondered where they all were but then remembered that it was Christmas and the staff had been allowed time off. The only sound she could hear was her own breathing and it comforted her to know she was alone. Taking a fortifying breath, she slowly walked down the stairs, dumping her bag at the bottom and then turned to the right down the hall. The door to his office was closed but with a determined breath, she opened it slowly, not exhaling until it was fully open and she saw that the room was empty. Taking slow measured steps, she walked over to the far end wall and stopped in front of an ornate wooden cabinet, opening it to reveal a safe. Gingerly, she went on her knees and punched in the code. Steven didn't know that she knew the combination, didn't know that her mother, drunk as a skunk and flying high on pills, had blurted it out, only to make her swear on her life not to mention anything to Steven. On well-oiled hinges, the door swung open silently, revealing its contents to her. She sat staring at several neatly stacked rows of cash, some documents and a slim pouch made from black velvet. Too wound up and frightened to be surprised at her find, she carefully took out the cash, amazed when she realised she was looking at well over fifty thousand dollars. She put the bundles to one side and pulled out the documents. After a quick glance at the papers, some political stuff she couldn't make sense of and some other correspondence that held no interest for her, she put them back. Finally, she grabbed the velvet pouch and pulled loose the drawstring holding it closed. The object within felt cylindrical and with sudden curiosity, she tipped it out with a gasp of surprise when she found herself holding what looked like a knife handle. Studying it for a moment, she found the silver button on the side of the handle and when she pressed it down, a seven-inch stainless-steel blade revealed itself. Carefully, she rand a finger down the sharp blade, staring at it. She had no idea what Steven was doing with such a thing, shuddering at the thought that he might have used it on her. Pushing the blade carefully back in its slot, she gathered the money and the knife before carefully closing the safe again and then left the office. She had to rearrange her bag to stuff all the cash into it but with a bit of shoving, she managed to close the zipper. The knife in her hand gave her a strange sense of security so she put the pouch in the back pocket of her jeans. Picking up the heavy bag, she winced as she threw the strap over her shoulder. Collecting her warm winter jacket, she slipped out of the house and into the night.

Chapter 1

Evie Templeton tapped away at her keyboard, fingers flying at an amazing speed as she finished what she was working on and let out a huff of satisfaction. Everything was set up to get all the necessary paperwork she would need in a couple of weeks. As always when she worked on illegal sites, she backtracked her steps, erasing all trace of her activity before shutting down her laptop. Stretching her arms above her head, she wriggled in her chair, trying to loosen the kinks out of her sore back. It had been a long day and an even longer night but now that she'd finished her latest assignment, she could take time to relax before she tackled the next one on her list. The past six months had been hard work but everything had gone exactly as she'd planned. Evie never left anything to chance, her prep work was a study in meticulous planning, double and triple checking all the facts before she acted. Peter Saunders had been no exception and Evie thought that, once again, she'd done well to execute the plan as perfectly as she had. Taking the time to set up everything, getting to know his habits, his life and work, she'd spent months figuring out the best way to get close enough to him to fulfil her assignment. The ease with which she'd accomplished it all came as no surprise. Peter Saunders was a small-time business man who ran a chain of drycleaners. At least that was what he showed the public. Behind the scenes he was a paedophile of the worst kind, his particular interest being girls between the ages of ten and fourteen. Evie had unearthed a wealth of information on his activities, not hard to do when you knew where to look and Evie knew just how to access all the information she needed. Being an accomplished hacker had its advantages and Evie was an expert. In this case, her hacking skills also revealed that Peter Saunders was in trouble with the IRS and was in desperate need of a good accountant who could help sort out the mess he was in. Evie had designed and printed a flier, announcing herself as a newly established accountant who was looking for new clients.

Dropping the leaflet into his letterbox, she'd waited, knowing that eventually he would call, because she'd made sure the "introductory offer" was a hook someone like him would swallow without too much thought. Men like him were always looking for a cheap deal and that was exactly what she'd offered. As predicted, two days after dropping the flyer, he'd called. Meeting him, Evie had slipped into the role of eager young account, complimenting him on the success of his business and generally making him feel a million dollars. Getting him to sign the contract had been like taking candy from a baby and Evie promised to sort out the mess he found himself in, even adding that there might be a chance he'd get some money back, because let's face it, the IRS was known for making mistakes, right? As predicted, he was lured by her promises and, after that initial meeting, he'd handed everything over to Evie. Looking at the mountain of receipts and accounts, all jumbled together in a card board box along with a generous payment as a first instalment, Evie smiled and promised to get back to him as soon as possible. At first, he'd been reluctant to hand over money before she'd done any work but Evie had detailed her need for some funds with such pity inducing tones, even batting her eye lashes at him, he'd coughed up the cash. She let him stew for a couple of weeks, fobbing him off with emails full of fake promises and asking him to please be patient whilst assuring him that everything was going well and that she'd have a report done shortly. Yesterday, that report had been ready and Evie had agreed to meet at his home to go over it in detail with him. Leaning back in her chair, she let her mind drift back to the events of the night.

She'd dressed carefully, her simple black suit and demure pink roll neck sweater giving the appearance of a serious business person, the leather messenger bag completing the look.

His house was on the small side but in a decent neighbourhood, a narrow concrete path leading up to a front door in need of a paint job. Evie didn't see a door bell so instead, she rapped on the door with her gloved hand. As if he had been waiting on the other side, the door opened immediately.

"Ms. Templeton, how lovely to see you!" He said, a smarmy grin on his face. "Please, come in, come in."

Keeping her smile plastered on her face, she shook his proffered hand and stepped into the hall of his mediocre home. He led her to the sitting area containing an old brown sofa, a cheap lamp and a seventies style coffee table, made from chipped Formica. Evie took off her leather gloves and stuffed them in her bag.

"Please have a seat." He said, pointing to the sofa. "Can I get you a drink?"

"No, thank you. I'm snowed under with work so I would prefer to go through the report with you straight away." She bit her lip for effect, indicating that she was nervous.

"Of course! Hope you don't mind if I fetch a beer for myself and then we can get started."

While he went down the hall to fetch his drink, Evie reached into her satchel and pulled out what she needed for the next step, placing a folder on the coffee table in front of her but keeping the small, rectangular black box in her hand, covering it with her bag.

"There we are!"

Peter Saunders said as he came back in the room, taking a seat next to her, eagerly looking at the file on the table. Evie picked up the folder and handed it to him, getting her other hand out from under her bag and, before he could even take hold of the folder, tasered him twice in quick succession. She watched as he fell to the ground, dropping his bottle as he lay twitching on the floor before passing out.

"Well, that went well, I feel." She looked at the man on the floor.

Calmly, she stood and pulled a pair of surgical gloves out of her bag, putting them on before proceeding to tie his hands and his ankles together behind his back with plastic zip ties.

"There, that should do!"

She smiled and walked back to the hall, leaving the hogtied man on the floor. She stripped out of her business suit and sweater, folding them neatly and placing them in a plastic bag. The skin-tight bodysuit she was left wearing had a belt attached to her waist with several pouches where she kept the few items she would need. Taking off her shoes, she placed them in the plastic bag with her clothes, slipping her feet into a pair of brand-new sneakers and then went back to the sitting room. Peter Saunders had stopped twitching but was still out cold which suited her fine. Dragging him into the bathroom was hard work, he wasn't a slim man and she was breathing heavily from the effort. She cut away his clothes, after all, he wouldn't be needing them again and threw them in his dirty linen hamper. Looking down at the disgusting naked form of the man she knew had abused young girls for many years, she pushed away the revulsion she felt and concentrated instead on the task in hand. It was quite a struggle to get the man into his bathtub, fat pig that he was but once he was placed half sitting up, she switched on the shower, dousing him with cold water. He came to, spluttering in confusion and probably still sore from the electric shook she'd sent through his system.

"What the . ."

Before he could say anything else, Evie stuffed a gag in his mouth, taping it securely in place. He tried to struggle but soon it became evident that he knew he was trapped. The look in his eyes showed his fear and Evie smiled.

"Well now, Peter, I think I owe you an explanation, don't you think?"

Her sarcastic tone was completely lost on him as he nodded eagerly. Evie sat down on the closed toilet lid and looked at him for a moment before unzipping one of the pouches on her suit, extracting a black velvet pouch. Pulling apart the drawstring, she let the folded knife slide into her hand. She watched his eyes grow big as he realised what she was holding, growing bigger still as she pressed the button to release the beautiful seven-inch steel slim blade. He tried to scream but the gag was doing its job and all that escaped was a muffled sound. Evie ran a gloved finger along the shiny blade, caressing it as if it was a pet.

"See Peter, I know all about you and your taste in young girls."

At her words he let out another muffled groan but Evie continued, ignoring his outburst.

"Sadly, for you, I cannot allow you to continue to live. But what I can and will do is to make sure you suffer, just like you made all those girls suffer, you sick fucker!"

In one fluid motion, she stood and plunged the blade in his abdomen just below the pubic bone and drew the blade down, cleanly slicing his flaccid pathetic dick in two. This time the muffled scream was louder, his face contorted with pain.

"Oh, I'm sorry, did that hurt?"

She looked down at him coldly, watching the tears stream down his face. Glancing at the wound she'd created, she saw a steady flow of blood running down his flabby thigh and into the white tub. Nodding to herself, she approached the tub again.

"Hmm ... not bad, I guess, but let's see how you feel about this."

With another swift motion, she drove the blade into his side, knowing exactly where to pierce to reach the liver, ensuring maximum blood loss but not so much that he'd die instantly. His eyes rolled into the back of his head for a moment, the muffled screams temporarily stopping.

"Oh no, you don't!" Evie switched on the shower, dowsing him with ice cold water until he opened his eyes again.

"There, that's better. Can't have you passing out just yet."

Raising the blade again, she carved a large X across his chest, making sure not to cut too deep. Marking him in this way was not intended to kill. Just her version of a final kiss.

Staring up at her, she looked into his eyes and saw the agony. Mortally wounded, it would take him a good while to bleed out and Evie was happy to let him die on his own. Turning, she carefully rinsed the blade in the sink and then pulled out a surgical wipe to clean the shiny blade before flipping it shut and slipping it back into its velvety home. She put the pouch back in the pocket of her suit, careful to close the zipper. Without looking at the dying man in the tub, she turned and left the bathroom. In the sitting room, she gathered the useless folder and her taser, placing the items back in her satchel. She pulled out a microfibre cloth and carefully wiped the table where she'd been sat. She didn't think she'd touched any of it but it paid to be thorough. She walked through the small house and soon found what passed for an office, his laptop conveniently open. She sat down and started typing, getting into his system easily because, let's face it, men like him were too tight to invest in a proper security program. Erasing all traces of her dealings with him, she closed the computer down and then rifled through the papers on his messy desk, smiling when she found the flyer and carefully pocketing it.

Back in the hall, she got dressed in her suit and sweater, picked up the plastic bag and stowed it away in her satchel. Glancing around, she was satisfied that she'd cleared all traces and opened the door, shutting it quietly behind her. Checking to make sure no one was around, she wiped the door panel where she'd knocked on the door earlier and then left.

Chapter 2

The insistent ringing of his phone woke Special Agent Lucas Green from sleep and with a practiced grab, he answered.

"Green"

"Morning Lucas, sorry to call so early."

The chirpy tone of his partner and fellow agent Dan Mortimer hit his ear. He looked at the clock on his bedside table and saw it was just before six which meant he'd had about four hours sleep.

"Fuck, Dan, this better be good!" He grumbled, holding the phone away from his ear to avoid hearing Dan's cheerful laugh.

"Come on you grumpy old bugger. I wouldn't be calling this early if it wasn't."

"Guess not" Lucas replied. "So, what have we got?"

"Another X murder, no less!" Dan's voice had lost its cheerful tone. Murder wasn't something to be joked about.

"What? Where?" Lucas shot out of bed, wide awake now and tried pulling his pants on with one hand, nearly toppling over.

"Shit! Hang on a minute, Dan!"

He put the phone down and pulled up his pants, adding a shirt before picking the phone up again.

"Shoot!"

"Some guy by the name of Peter Saunders, found late last night. Neighbours complained that there was a weird smell coming from the back of the property so the cops forced open the door and found him in his bathtub." Dan paused a moment.

"Apparently, he was carved up, the standard X on his chest making him victim number six, dammit!"

Lucas swore under his breath. The X killer, as he'd been dubbed by the press, had struck all across the country, always leaving the same mark on his victims, just in case the cops were too stupid to link the victims. After the second victim had been found six years ago, the FBI had gotten involved but they were no nearer to finding the bastard now than they had been all those years ago. There was not a single trace of any kind of evidence, no DNA, no finger prints, nothing. It was frustrating as hell and Lucas knew, that if the killer didn't slip up this time, they wouldn't find anything useful at the new crime scene either. The guy was just too good to leave anything behind. With a sigh, he asked for the crime scene address and arranged to meet Dan there.

"And for God's sake, pick up some damn coffee!" He growled before hanging up.

Half an hour later, he pulled up in front of the house, pleased to see that the cops had cordoned off the entire front of the house and were busy keeping a small crowd of onlookers at bay. Dan stood chatting with one of the uniforms but turned at his approach, holding out the requested coffee. He handed Lucas a pair of disposable boot covers and then lifted the crime scene tape to approach the house. Lucas took a large gulp of the coffee and then followed Dan up the narrow path and squeezed past a CSI guy who was busy dusting the door for prints. Once inside, he slipped on his boot covers and followed Dan down the small hall into the bathroom.

The scene was quite gruesome, dried blood had congealed against the bloated corps of one Peter Saunders. The small bathroom window was open as fully as it would go but still, the stench was awful. Lucas wasn't too fazed by it, he'd attended too many crime scenes to let it bother him much but that didn't mean he liked it. Looking at Dan, who was a few years younger and maybe not quite as seasoned as Lucas, he saw that his partner was having a hard time dealing with the smell.

"Breathe through your mouth, it's not so bad then." He advised him with a look of sympathy before turning back to the tub. Bent over the victim was Ben Foster, the local coroner. Looking up as Lucas and Dan entered the small bathroom, he gave them a grim smile.

"Hey guys, we've got a ripe one here!" He stood up and put away his tools.

"Been dead about two days I'd say but I'll let you know for sure once I've got him on the table." Ben paused for a moment, a frown on his ebony forehead.

"Dammit, Lucas, how many are there now?"

Lucas sighed and ran a hand over his stubbled chin. He'd had no time to shave this morning.

"Six, unless the sick bastard didn't mark all of his victims."

"Let's hope you're right!" Ben shook his head, taking another look at the dead man in the tub.

"He didn't die easily." He said quietly. "Bled out over a couple of hours. The killer certainly knows how to inflict maximum pain without actually killing outright."

"Sick fuck!" Dan muttered and Lucas nodded in agreement.

"Are you finished with him, Ben?"

The coroner nodded. "Yeah, CSI have taken pictures so he can be moved. I'll be in touch once I've finished with him."

All three men left the bathroom and once outside in the fresh air, Lucas took a deep breath to clear his lungs of the stench of death from the tiny bathroom.

A few hours later, Lucas was staring at the five other files related to the X murderer. There was plenty to link all the victims, not only because they had all been marked with an X but all of them were paedophiles and Lucas knew, the killer saw himself as some kind of sick vigilante who thought he was doing the world a favour by getting rid of them. It pissed him off that these guys had escaped justice for their crimes. In his opinion, there was nothing worse than child abusers but still, he wanted these sorts of perps brought to justice to rot in jail for the rest of their days. Killing them seemed too good for what they had done to defenceless kids, even dying in the horrible ways they all had and it made him mad as hell that they had no leads as to who was responsible for killing them. Dan entered the office with a small grin on his face.

"What have you got to smile about?" Lucas asked, still feeling pissed off.

"Well now, I just heard back from Joe, the IT guy. He's had a look at the victim's laptop and guess what? Someone has accessed it two days ago, erasing data!"

Lucas was dumbstruck for a moment.

"Can he recover it?" Hope rang clear in his question.

Dan shrugged and sat down at his desk.

"He's going to try. He's relatively new in the Bureau but he came highly recommended and is a bit of a whizz by all accounts. Let's hope he finds something other than the links to some seriously sick websites because the CSI guys have found nothing! Not a damn thing, as per!" Dan let out a frustrated huff.

"Joe has passed the info of the sites to other agents who deal with kiddie porn. At the very least they'll shut them down so I guess that's something."

Scratching his head, Lucas went back to studying the files in front of him. The victims had been spread right across the country, one in Texas, one in Colorado, another one in Kentucky and two in Ohio. And now, victim number six here in Baltimore. All were male, aged between forty and sixty-five and, apart from the Kentucky victim, all had been single or divorced. Looking at the crime scene pictures, they had been made to suffer, albeit in various ways but Lucas understood Ben's comment about the killer knowing what he was doing because the stab wounds had one thing in common. Inflict maximum pain but ensuring a slow death, either through piercing the liver, as was the case with victim number six or a well-placed blade in the kidneys or lungs. On one occasion, the killer had actually opened the veins on both arms of the victim, number three if he remembered correctly, making sure to cut vertically but not too far to slow the eventual bleed out. Yeah, he knew what he was doing alright. Lucas wondered, and not for the first time, if the killer had some medical training? He certainly knew where the high impact spots were on a human body to induce a slow death! With a frustrated sigh, he closed the files. His stomach reminded him that he hadn't eaten all day and since he wasn't getting anywhere with work, he might as well go and eat. His phone interrupted thoughts of food.

"Green."

"Lucas, it's Ben. I would like you and Dan to come down and have a look at your vic."

"Why?"

"Because I've found something I think might be of interest."

"And you can't tell me over the phone?" He knew he was being a grouch but couldn't help himself.

"I would prefer to show you."

Lucas wasn't a fan of autopsies but something in Ben's voice made him put his dislike to one side.

"Sure, whatever. We're on our way." He hung up and turned to Dan who had been listening to his side of the conversation.

"Where are we going?"

"That was Ben. He wants us to go and have a look at the victim. Apparently, there might be some stuff that could be useful."

Dan pulled a face. "Why can't he put it in his report? I was hoping to get home before the kids are in bed."

"Sorry, pal." Lucas clapped a sympathetic hand on his shoulder.

Once at the morgue, they found Ben waiting for them, the body on the table in front of him covered by a sheet with only the head visible.

"Thank you for coming down, gentlemen." Ben grinned when he saw Dan pulling a face. "I promise I'll make it worth your while."

Chuckling, he pulled down the sheet covering the corpse, revealing the chest with the large X carved on it and motioned for them to step closer. Pointing a gloved hand to a place just below the sternum, he waited for them to see what he saw. Lucas stepped a little closer and, looking at where Ben's finger was pointing, noticed two small red marks.

"What are these?" He asked, eyebrows raised in question.

Dan also approached the table, the same question clearly evident on his face.

"Those, my friends, are Taser wounds." Ben let the statement hang in the air, waiting for their reaction.

"Fuck me!" Dan let out a surprised huff. "He was tasered?"

"Yep" Ben said, grinning. "I told you it would be of interest, didn't I?"

Lucas understood exactly what Ben was saying, though Dan took a little longer before he got it.

"Now I get it!" He exclaimed, scratching the stubble on his chin. "I've been wondering how the hell the murderer managed to get the man into the bath without a struggle. Of course, if he was unconscious at the time, that would make things easier."

Lucas nodded, having had the exact same thoughts. "Yeah, it's not that he's particularly tall but he must weigh a bit?"

He looked over at Ben.

"350 to be precise." The coroner grinned.

"Well I'll be damned! But still, our killer must be a strong guy. Imagine having to shift 350 pounds of dead weight and then putting him in the tub." Dan sounded quite impressed, despite the grim topic.

Shaking his head, Lucas tried to get a mental picture of the killer. He was strong, certainly, but Lucas also knew there were ways to carry an unconscious person, firemen did it all the time. He himself had once carried an unconscious fellow soldier from the explosion site of an IUD. He'd been a fairly decent size man and well-muscled. Lucas had hoisted him over his shoulder, part of the upper body of the unconscious man resting on his back pack. The weight had been distributed over a greater area, therefore making it a little easier. Still, it was no mean feat to get a man that size into a tub.

"I'd say so." Ben interjected, before pulling the sheet back over the corpse. "Anyway, I'll have my report ready for tomorrow. Now, if you'll excuse me, my wife is waiting for me. It's date night tonight."

He added the last with a dramatic sigh, although judging by the wide smile on his face, it wasn't exactly a chore.

Grinning, Lucas and Dan left and as they stood waiting for the elevator to take them back up to street level, Lucas's stomach gave a loud growl. Dan looked at him and burst out laughing.

"What? I haven't eaten all day, I'm starved! Want to go and get pizza?" Lucas grinned.

Dan nodded. "Sounds like a plan."

He cast an eye at his watch and pulled a face.

"I've missed dinner with Marie and the twins anyway so you'll do fine as an eating partner. As long as you don't expect me to pick up the tab we're good!" He added with a wink.

Lucas laughed and did up the zipper on his jacket. It was freezing outside.

Chapter 3

Evie walked along the aisles of her local Deli, wondering what to get for dinner, browsing the goods on offer and not really paying attention to her surroundings. As always after an assignment was complete, her mind was a little hazy as a sense of accomplishment filled her. It usually took her several days to get her head clear again and after the last one, she definitely needed a break. While deciding where she wanted to go, she would spend a few days holed up in her apartment and for that she needed food. Once her shopping was complete, she would not venture out again until she decided where her next assignment would be. There was no question of going off for a relaxing holiday until she knew where she'd be going next. Thoughts of one particular project tried to invade her mind but she pushed them away, not ready to even contemplate that particular target. Instead, she filled her trolley with goodies and then proceeded to the check-out. She was just about to leave the store after picking up her bags when her eye caught the headline of one of the many glossy magazines lining the shelves behind the check-out. As she tried to comprehend what she was seeing, the bags dropped from her arms, crashing to the floor and she had to reach out and hang on to the shelf to stop herself from following her groceries on the floor. It couldn't be!! Staring at the glossy magazine, she saw a face from the past grinning at her, her heart beat tripling in seconds and she fought to bring air into her lungs. The picture showed a man standing next to a woman, both of them very well dressed and expertly put together, their happy smiles beaming from their faces. But it wasn't that that had her in such turmoil. It was the young girl standing next to the couple, barely a teenager, smiling shily at the camera, her long blonde hair braided and falling across her shoulder.

Senator Heffner and his fiancée, Whitney Porter, along with her daughter Rachel are getting ready for their big day!

The headline screamed at her, making her dizzy with a fear so intense, she thought she was going to black out!

"Miss? Are you alright?"

A voice brought her out of her stupor and Evie turned to see the cashier looking at her with concern in her eyes.

"What? Yes, yes I'm fine" she stuttered. "Sorry, just had a bit of a dizzy spell there."

Pull yourself together, she told herself firmly, taking a deep breath and schooling her features.

"I think I'll take a copy of this as well." She said and handed the cashier the magazine, fishing out some cash from her bag and then picked up her groceries off the floor. She saw the woman looking at her again, clearly wondering whether she would manage to stay upright.

"Colin!"

The woman shouted towards the back of the store.

"Come and give this lady a hand with her bags." Evie watched as a gangly teenager came ambling down the aisle, a friendly smile on his face.

"Let me take these for you, Miss." He said and took the bags from her arms.

"Thank you!" Evie gave him a grateful smile and followed him out of the store after having thanked the woman behind the check-out.

Making her way to her car took all the strength she had left and after the boy had stowed away her bags, she slumped in her car seat, too shocked to move for what seemed like hours. Unable to process what she'd just experienced and despite her best efforts, it took her a long time to get control over the panic that threatened to stop her heart. Finally, with shaking hands, she started the car and made her way back to her apartment.

Getting home and putting away the groceries, Evie felt as if she was in a dream, no make that a nightmare! Any notion she'd had about eating were long gone as she sat at the small kitchen table, staring at the magazine in front of her. Memories tried to surface, recollections of the pain and suffering she'd endured threatened to overwhelm her and with a sob, she flung the magazine off the table, sending it flying into the small living room where it landed on the floor face down. Shaking uncontrollably, Evie got up and opened her fridge, grabbed the half empty bottle of Tequila and put the bottle to her lips without bothering to get a glass. Taking a couple of large gulps, she felt the burn of the liquor spreading heat on its way down to her stomach. Swaying a little from the impact of the burn, she sat back down, placing the bottle in front of her and sat staring at it for a while. The alcohol found its way into her system and helped to calm her somewhat. Holding out her hands, she saw that they had finally stopped shaking, her breathing returning back to a more normal speed as she pushed her sweat soaked hair away from her face before taking another large gulp. With a sigh, she put the bottle back in the fridge. It would do her no good to get drunk, she knew from experience that alcohol was only a temporary solution and not a very good one at that. Over the years, she had learned to keep the nightmare inducing memories at bay by boxing them up, firmly closing the lid and storing them away in the furthest recesses of her mind. Usually, that worked well enough, only after completing an assignment did the nightmares make a brief return before she regained control. In the beginning, Evie had spent months in a dark fog of despair, flitting from place to place, never staying anywhere for long. Gradually, as her physical health improved, she had found solace in learning everything there was to find on the net about coding, hacking and other, mostly illegal, stuff. Whilst still at school, Maths had been her favourite subject and she'd always had a knack for finding her way around computers. Her IT teacher had been impressed by her abilities and had encouraged her, even going so far as to give her extra tuition on coding. Numbers had a calming influence on her and the ordered beauty of a complex code or mathematical problem helped focus her mind. Becoming an expert hacker had been a natural progression, once she had the basics, her natural flair had taken over. Reading and writing code was as easy for her as reading a book and so what if most of it was illegal, she didn't care. She used her talent as she saw fit, she had no one to answer to. Creating new identities, hacking into rich people's accounts and even richer fat cat corporations to take a slice of their fortunes without being detected was a game she enjoyed and so far, no one had caught up with her. These days, she seldom hacked for profit, the money she had obtained illegally during the first few years had been invested and she wasn't short of cash anymore. Along with money came the security she craved. She was independent, relying on no one but herself and therefore no one would be able to take it all away. It never occurred to her that her existence wasn't normal, that the life she'd created for herself was that of a lone wolf. It was exactly what she wanted and given her assignments, it was the only way she could operate.

Feeling calmer now, she picked up the magazine off the floor and turned it over. She opened it and found herself staring down at a series of glossy pictures of the happy couple in their home, getting ready to tie the knot in a month's time. The gushing report detailed how the Senator had known his future wife for many years but it was at a fund raiser in DC that he'd realised just how special she was. Although unwilling to forget about his first wife who had tragically died ten years ago, he hadn't been able to stop himself from falling in love with the beautiful Whitney and her adorable daughter. He said that he felt ready to begin living again, a feat that he hadn't thought possible.

Evie felt her stomach turn as she read the words and ran to the bathroom just in time to bring up what little there was left in her stomach from breakfast. Sliding onto the cold bathroom tiles, she sat, stunned at what she'd just seen. The bastard! Was he going to do it again? Had he been doing it all these years to God knows who?? Her mind whirled in a mad circle of thoughts and memories, her now empty stomach trying to heave again but she pushed a hand over her mouth and tried to breathe through it. She suddenly realised there had been no mention of her in the article and for the first time ever, she wondered what explanation he'd given regarding her disappearance. Then again, she hadn't had many friends and no other family. Even before her mother's death, a tragic car accident apparently, yeah right, she'd been reluctant to bring school friends home during the holidays. Although it was never said out loud, such visits wouldn't have been welcome, her mother more often than not either drunk or off her face on drugs. Not something you shared with your classmates, girls from privileged backgrounds, who were boarding with her at an expensive school. These girls wouldn't have understood and she had been too ashamed to say anything anyway. Discussing such private matters wasn't an option, particularly in a world of political ambition, where appearance was everything. Therefore, coming up with a plausible explanation would not have been that difficult for him. Memories crowded her, making her head spin.

Chapter 4

"Sweetie, I want you to meet someone today." Her mother smiled at her.

"Who is it, Mama?" Her mother took her hand and sat down on the sofa, pulling her into her lap.

"You know how your Daddy is in heaven, looking down at us, making sure we're okay?"

Her eight-year old self nodded with a smile.

"Yes, I do, Mama."

Of course, she knew! Her Daddy had been a very brave man, Mama had told her when she'd been old enough to understand. He'd been a soldier who had given his own life so that many others didn't have to die. She had no memories of him since he'd gone to heaven before she'd been born but her Mama had lots of pictures and they often spent many hours looking at them while Mama would tell her how they had met. She loved that story about her Daddy the best because Mama's eyes would light up at the memory as she recounted how her Daddy had been so kind and loving, how excited he'd been when they had found out, they were going to have a baby. But despite all that, she often wished she'd have a real Daddy, one who would play with her and take her on outings. Sometimes, when her friends from school talked about the fun they were having with their Dads, she felt sad that she didn't have one too.

"Well, how would you feel if you were to get another Daddy?" Her mother looked at her in question, her blue eyes exactly the same as her own.

"Another Daddy?" She didn't understand what her Mama was saying.

"Yeah, you know, so you would get to do all the fun stuff your friends get to do with their Daddies."

She looked at her mother, a smile spreading across her little face as she thought just how much she would love that.

"Really?"

Smiling, her mother nodded. "Yes, really. You see, I've met this really nice man. His name is Steven and he would just love to meet you."

She thought about that for a moment. It would be wonderful but what if he didn't like her? Frowning, she looked at her mother.

"Do you think he'll like me?"

Her mother hugged her close, kissing her and stroking her hair. "Of course he's going to like you! How could he not? You're the most wonderful girl in the world!"

Comforted by her Mama's reassurances, her smile returned.

"Will I get a new dress?" She wanted to make a good impression on this man. If he was going to be her new Daddy, she was sure, a new dress would help.

"Yes!" Her mother laughed, hugging her again. "How about we go shopping? We'll meet Steven for dinner and of course, for that we need new outfits!"

They'd had so much fun, picking out clothes ready for their very first dinner with her new Daddy. They were to meet up in an exclusive restaurant, her mother had told her that she would have to remember her table manners, just like she'd been taught. Promising to be on her best behaviour, she was going to do everything she could to get her new Daddy to like her. On the night, she'd been enchanted with Steven, he'd been so lovely, asking her about her favourite toys and about school. She'd told him excitedly that she loved school, they even got to wear a special uniform, with it being a private school. Steven seemed suitably impressed by that. Then she told him how much she loved her pony, riding around the extensive grounds of their home, helping Joshua, the groom, taking care of her.

"Her name is Daisy" she said. "She's black with a white star on her forehead and she's really sweet and I have never fallen off!"

Taking a breath, she gave him a triumphant smile.

"I'm impressed, princess." Steven grinned. "I look forward to meeting her."

Her mother had watched the interaction between them, a happy smile lighting up her beautiful face.

A year later, her mother had married Steven and they'd moved to a new house. Her mother had explained to a tearful nine-year old that unfortunately, they wouldn't be able to bring Daisy as the new house didn't have stabling facilities.

"I won't move, not without Daisy!" Life without her childhood friend was unthinkable. Her mother put her arms around her as she sobbed.

"Listen sweetheart, how about we find a really nice riding school for you to go to?"

She shook her head. "I don't want to go to a stupid riding school! I want to keep Daisy!"

"We can't take her with us, honey. Steven's house does not have stable facilities, it's in the city."

Her mother sighed, her voice gentle. "You wouldn't be able to ride Daisy for much longer anyway, you're getting to be too big for her. Maybe in the new riding school, you could start to ride a horse instead of a pony."

She looked at her mother in shocked surprise. "Well, I can still ride her and I don't want to move to the stupid city. I'll just stay here with Annie and Joshua. That way I get to keep Daisy and you don't have to find anywhere else."

Crossing her arms over her small chest, she looked at her mother with a triumphant smile on her face. Her mother smiled but shook her head.

"You can't stay here, sweetie."

"Why not? I stay with Annie and Joshua when you're away. I love them and they love me!" Desperation clawed at her, the increasingly scary feeling that her mother was going to refuse her made her heart race.

"Darling, listen to me!" Her mother's voice was not quite as gentle as before.

"You can't stay here because I have sold the house and Annie and Joshua are retiring. And anyway, you belong with me. I couldn't possibly leave you behind."

Her mother reached a hand out to her but she pulled away, fresh tears running down her cheeks. Her mother's words echoed inside her head but she simply refused to hear them. Anger rose swiftly and she lashed out.

"I hate you and I hate Steven! I wish I wasn't your daughter!"

With an angry sob she turned and ran, seeking sanctuary in the stable where Daisy stood patiently as her coat grew wet with tears.

Just as her mother had said, the house was sold, their belongings packed up and despite her pleading, Daisy was fetched by her new owners the day before they were due to move to Steven's home. Of course, she hadn't known then that this was only the beginning, hadn't realised that the happiness she'd known when it had been just her and her mother was ending. Gradually, almost without her realising it, her mother became distant, often having to accompany Steven to some function or other and spending large chunks of time on various Charity committees. When she'd asked her mother why they never had time anymore to do fun things together, she'd been told that it was very important that her mother was seen in the right circles because of Steven's career. Promises to make time for her, once his political ambitions had been achieved, never materialised. Instead, she noticed her mother losing weight, she also seemed to have issues with coordination and a certain amount of memory loss. When prompted about a promise to spend time together, she would claim to have no knowledge of any such conversation, scolding her for being selfish.

"Grow up!" Her mother once told her after a particularly heated exchange. "The world does not revolve around you, my girl! I think Steven is right about sending you to boarding school, you're far too much of a handful these days."

She'd been shipped off to a very exclusive school, hundreds of miles away, abandoned by her mother and sacrificed for the career of an egotistical man. From that day on, she hated Steven. She knew he'd made her mother change because the woman parading as her mother showed no resemblance to the loving and warm Mama she'd once had. Only allowed home during the long summer holidays, she was forced to spend her days at home, still alone since her mother seemed not to care one way or another if she was there or not. She kept out of the way as much as possible, even more so when she'd discovered that not only was her mother a drunk, she was also doing some heavy-duty pill popping, altering her personality to that of a complete stranger. Steven was seldom at home but when he was, she was forced to sit at the dinner table, trying in vain to force food down her throat. The fact that she pushed her food around her plate rather than eat it caused endless rows which usually ended with her mother storming out, leaving her alone with him. Ignoring her completely, he would finish his meal and then leave, finally allowing her to breathe freely for the first time since the start of the meal.

She'd been away at school when the news had come that her mother had been killed in a car crash. The head mistress had expressed her condolences and told her that she would be allowed to go home for the funeral, asking her if there was anything she needed help with. Refusing politely, she'd accepted the woman's expression of sympathy at the loss of her mother but to her, her Mama had died a long time ago. Arriving home, she was greeted by the housekeeper, who told her that Steven was still in DC. She didn't see or hear from him until the day before the funeral. She was in her room, reading, when she heard him come in, talking to someone. Creeping down the stairs and hiding behind a large planter standing to one side of the hall, she listened to the men talking in Steven's office.

"Fucking drunk again, was she?"

She knew the man's voice very well. He was a friend of Steven, they were always together, doing God knows what. In one of her more lucid moments, long before her death, her mother had explained that the man, Daniel Porter, was Stevens' right-hand man, helping him with his campaign to become Senator.

"Of course!" Steven sneered. "How the fuck are we going to explain this pile of shit? If this gets out, I can kiss good bye any notion of running another campaign ever again!"

She heard the clinking of ice cubes and then liquid being poured.

"Don't worry, my friend, I've got this." Daniel now said. "I've got some good connections in the Police force. We'll bury this shit so deep, no one will ever find it again. We can spin the whole thing to your advantage."

"How so?" Steven sounded unconvinced.

"Well, just think! Grieving widower, left to look after the brat, playing at being Super Dad to make sure the poor girl doesn't go off the rails because of the tragic loss of her beloved mother!"

Daniel laughed at his own ingenuity. "I can just see the headlines! I'm telling you, this will work out great. After a decent time of mourning, you'll ship the kid off back to school and you're home and dry."

And that was exactly what had happened. The next time she'd come home, it had been for the Christmas holidays. The house had been bare, no decorations had been put up, due to the death of her mother. The housekeeper had told her that Steven had given strict instructions about that. He wanted nothing to remind him that his dear wife was no longer here to celebrate the Holidays with them. Of course, she knew better but didn't say anything. The day after Christmas, he'd raped her.

Of course, many years later she'd realised that Steven had married her mother for her money. Mama came from a wealthy family and, being an only child, had inherited everything after the death of her parents. Such wealth was what Steven had needed to back his campaigns, marrying into money had been the simplest option, an easy way to fund his ambitious career plans.

She looked at the pictures again, studying the woman who stood next to the Senator. She seemed familiar, somehow. But that couldn't be, could it? She knew she'd never met the woman or her daughter. And then it hit her. It wasn't the woman's face that was familiar but her name! Whitney Porter and her daughter Rachel! Evie jumped up and fetched her laptop, opened her browser and typed in the woman's name. Bingo! Whitney Porter, widow of Daniel Porter, Steven's righthand man, who'd spoken about her mother as if she was just a piece of trash. Daniel Porter had met his end almost identically to her mother. He'd died in a car crash, and although nothing was mentioned in the official version, it didn't take Evie long to find other articles, items that had been supressed from being published by a court order. Stories of drug taking and rumours of infidelity, being seen visiting high end vice dens. The list went on and on. Although she felt sorry for the little girl who had lost her Dad, she was glad he was dead. And now, Whitney was marrying the Senator! Was this political matchmaking or was Whitney really in love with him? She knew Steven wasn't capable of loving anyone but himself so it couldn't be a real love match. Searching further into Whitney's background, Evie found the reason. Whitney had money, lots of it and if that wasn't enough for Steven to propose, she didn't know what was. History was repeating itself and she felt sick all over again. But this time, she would be there to stop him, she wouldn't let him destroy another woman's life, let alone that of a little girl.

With renewed determination she got up and washed her face, staring at her reflection in the mirror for a long time. Her complexion had an unhealthy paleness from the shock, dark circles cast a shadow beneath her piercing green eyes, her red hair, darkened by sweat, stuck to her head. Realisation hit her with brutal force. This was it then, time to get her head into the end game. In the back of her mind Evie had always known this day would come but had refused to even think about what that would entail. Over the years, she had avoided thinking about all of this but seeing the pictures, she knew she had no choice now, knew what she needed to do. He was always going to be her last, just as he'd been her first. Panic at the thought of what was to come threatened to overwhelm her. It took a long time to even out her breathing, only the will to see this through to the bitter end making it possible to control the surge of panic. She needed a break. Right now, she was in no fit state to think about dealing with the Senator. Going away for a few days to regroup was the right thing to do. She needed time to recover from the shock and then, once her head was clear again, she would start planning her last assignment. With a last look at her own reflection, she stripped off her clothes and set the shower running. She needed to cleanse herself, not just her body but also her mind and a shower was as good a start as any.

Feeling much better after a long hot shower and dressed in clean clothes, Evie grabbed her laptop and settled on the sofa, ready to search for a small bit of paradise in which she could recover. Two hours later she was booked to spend a week on a tiny Caribbean island, leaving the following afternoon. With a heavy sigh, she went to pack her bags. As Evie pulled out summer dresses, bikinis and several pairs of sandals, she pushed thoughts of what lay ahead after her return from her mind.

After a leisurely breakfast the following morning, Evie logged on and checked that her requests had been acknowledged and completed. She sent a return message to arrange collection the following week, then backtracked and erased her steps before shutting down the system. Glancing at the cell phone lying beside the computer, she grabbed it, prised open the back cover, removing the battery and SIM card, cutting the latter neatly in two before flushing them down the toilet. She would throw the phone itself in a trash can at the airport. This was the last link to Peter Saunders, he obviously had to have her cell number and had called several times. Evie couldn't afford to let those calls be traced back to her. With a shrug, she put the phone in her bag. After next week, Evie Templeton would cease to exist and no one would find any trace of her ever having been here. The real Evie Templeton had died 4 years ago after complications following surgery in a hospital in New Jersey.

Chapter 5

Ten days into the investigation and still nothing! Lucas Green cursed and threw down the file he'd been reading for the tenth time, frustrated as hell at not getting anywhere. He dragged a hand through his dark hair, thinking he needed to get a visit to the barbers organised, judging by the feel of it. The initial excitement at the possibility of finding a trace to the killer from the victim's laptop had pretty much died a death since Joe, their best IT guy, had been unable to find anything at all that could have helped them with the investigation. Apparently, whoever had accessed the system knew what they were doing. Any traces had been cleaned up and there was no way of recovering anything. Not only was the killer knowledgeable about how to hurt people, apparently, he was also some kind of computer genius which was just peachy! How were they ever going to catch the bastard? No prints, no DNA and no anything else left them with precisely nothing to go on and that frustrated the shit out of Lucas. He cast a weary glance at his watch, realising it was well after six and decided to call it a day. He looked across the desk to find Dan tapping away at his computer, writing up a report. He too looked tired, they had both been working hard trying to get any kind of sense from what little information they had. Interviewing neighbours, work colleagues and friends of Peter Saunders had proved to be a waste of effort. None of the neighbours had heard anything during the night in question. Since there had been no sign of forced entry at the scene, both Lucas and Dan were sure that Peter had known his killer and had therefore opened the door without reservation or fear. That left them with the huge task of combing through any contacts the victim had been known to have, starting with the staff at his chain of five dry cleaning shops. Most of the twenty employees had already been ruled out of the investigation as they had solid alibis. Out of the four that were left, two were unable to provide an alibi as they lived alone and both the women had insisted that they were innocent. Lucas wouldn't rule either of them out altogether but given that the majority of serial killers were male and not fifty plus women trying to earn a living by doing other peoples' laundry, he didn't think he was not doing his job by not probing any further. One of the other employees was on holiday but was due back in a couple of days. That left one, a delivery guy named Michael Connor, whose whereabouts were currently unknown. According to records, he'd worked for Saunders for two years, delivering cleaned items to some of the better off clients. Initially, Dan had been quite excited by this development until they found out that up until he started working for Saunders, Connor had been in prison for assault. This put him firmly out of the frame as the first three murders had taken place while he was doing time. Wherever he was, he had nothing to do with the demise of his boss but Lucas had asked the local cops to keep an eye out for him anyway. Friends of the deceased, such as they were, couldn't help shed any light on the events either. Peter Saunders had not been a popular guy, the few names they had found in his cell phone had resulted in officers being despatched to interview them. Joe had been up earlier and had made a shit day even shittier with his news.

"So, this last contact, an E. Templeton" he started.

Both Lucas and Dan waited for him to continue.

"I've checked pretty much everywhere and the only E. Templeton I could find is an eighty-six-year-old man living in a nursing home." He paused for a moment. "I may not be a detective but I think we can rule him out as our killer." Joe grinned at his own comment.

"So, what are you saying?" Dan asked, frustration evident in his voice.

"I'm saying this person doesn't exist."

"What?" Lucas couldn't believe what he was hearing. "What the hell does that mean?"

Joe shrugged his skinny shoulders. "Exactly that. There are no other listings anywhere for an E. Templeton. The number on the victim's phone is a burner phone and it's no longer active."

At that, Lucas sat up straighter.

"Has to be the killer!"

Dan piped up from his desk and Lucas nodded in agreement. That was exactly what he'd been thinking too. But with no clue other than a non-existent name, they were still no further than before. It was frustrating as hell.

"Well, shit! Thanks anyway, Joe."

Lucas slumped in his chair, feeling deflated. Every time they thought they had something, the killer seemed to be one step ahead and frankly, that pissed him off. Lucas knew he needed to find a new angle to this investigation and to his mind, the clues had to be in the fact that all six victims had been paedos. He'd spent the last week checking the files to see if any of them had used the same websites to get their kicks, trying to figure out if any of them had had any contact with each other. It was a well know fact that these perverts formed some sort of close knit community, knowing full well that if one of them went down, others could follow so they protected their own kind whenever possible. He got Dan to liaise with the agents dealing with the sites, hoping that they could find the missing link. They were still waiting to hear.

"Hey Dan! Let's call it a day, yeah?"

Dan stopped typing and looked over at him, dragging a hand across his tired features.

"Yeah, this report can wait until tomorrow." Getting up, he grabbed his jacket.

"Fancy a drink?" Lucas asked but Dan shook his head.

"Sorry, not tonight. I kinda just need to spend some QT with Marie and the kids." He let out a huff.

"I've not been home much these past few days and haven't really spent any time with them."

"Sure, no problem."

Lucas smiled, feeling a little disappointed but he understood his partner. If he had a family to go home to, he wouldn't be contemplating going to a bar to try and forget the whole situation for a few hours either. Once upon a time, he too had been married but it had lasted only a couple of years. Both had realised that it wasn't working for either of them, a fact that had made the divorce fairly amicable; luckily, he and Stacey had no children to fight over. In the end, they had parted ways and the last he had heard from her was that she was in sunny California, where she had married again. That had been over six years ago. Since then, Lucas had never really found anyone to have a long-term relationship with, the occasional hook ups provided an opportunity to let off steam. It kept things simple, both he and the woman in question knew what to expect and thus avoid disappointment. It worked for him, he was married to the job and now, four years away from forty, he no longer felt the need to try and settle down and start a family. That ship had sailed a long time ago and he was content with that.

"Have a good evening. I'll see you tomorrow." Dan waved and disappeared down the corridor.

Lucas grabbed his own jacket and made his way to the underground parking. Once in his car, he debated where to go to drown his woes. For some reason, his regular sports bar didn't hold any appeal and on the spur of the moment, he decided to head downtown to one of the better hotels. He'd suited up this morning for a meeting with a Profiler to see what they could come up with. Under normal circumstances, he wouldn't have bothered with a suit but several of the top brass had been part of the meeting, wanting an update from Lucas, including his boss. The media were kicking up a storm and they needed something they could feed to the waiting press without giving away any important details about the investigation. It was bad enough the press had found out that Saunders was victim number six of the X murderer and Lucas really would have liked to find out how they knew. As far as the people in charge were concerned, all that mattered now was to get the media off their backs for a while. Lucas had nothing of any value and had therefore suggested the Profiler. The media hounds loved that kind of thing, it was something they could get their teeth into, speculating until the end of time without actually achieving anything. So, the Profiler had been brought in and sure enough, all things pointed to a male, probably white, perhaps Ex-Army, given that he seemed to have some knowledge of the human anatomy as well as being computer savvy. Age was estimated at between thirty and forty-five, certainly a loner, given that he killed right across the country. The profiler had promised to have his report ready by tomorrow but Lucas didn't expect much more than what had already been discussed.

Chapter 6

Pulling up outside one of downtowns' better hotels, he handed his keys to the valet and made his way into the hotel bar. Since it was still early, the bar was almost empty and the bartender took his order for a beer quickly. Taking the first sip, Lucas sat staring at the small bowl of complementary peanuts placed on the bar in front of him, his mind still on the case. For some reason, something was bothering him about all of it. Although the profiler had been cautious, he had confirmed the preliminary outlines of his report. And yet, Lucas had a gut feeling that they were missing a very important piece in this fucked up puzzle, though what that piece was, he hadn't a clue. Frustrated, he drained his beer and ordered another. While waiting for his beer, he cast a glance around the bar, which by now was beginning to fill up with workers stopping for a quick drink before heading home and Lucas saw a few unattached females glancing in his direction, clearly debating whether or not to approach him. He didn't feel inclined to encourage any attempts at making contact, letting his gaze drift. He was just about to turn back to the bar to grab his beer when a woman caught his attention. She was walking into the bar alone and, judging by the closed off look on her face, she wasn't in the mood for idle chat either. He watched her approach the bar, her long dark hair done in a simple yet elegant braid, hanging down over her left shoulder. She wore a well-cut black suit and a simple, pale pink silk top. Not overly tall, Lucas put her at around five seven, she was slim without appearing skinny. Her skin had a healthy glow as if she'd just come back from far sunnier climes than rainy Baltimore in October. Her voice was quiet but firm as she ordered her drink and he was surprised by her choice. He'd half expected her to order a colourful cocktail complete with a paper umbrella instead of a twelve-year old Scotch, no ice. He watched as she drank it down in one, then asking for a refill. Impressed, he wondered what had happened to her day to make her knock back Whiskey like that.

"Bad day at the office?" The words were out of his mouth before he realised.

The woman turned and cast a cold look at him, one elegant brow raised, clearly not amused by his question.

"No." She said curtly before downing the second drink and turning away, effectively cutting him off.

Normally, Lucas would have taken the hint but he had a sudden urge to find out what was bothering the beautiful woman standing next to him.

"Want another?" he asked, waiting to see her reaction. He didn't have to wait long.

"Listen, I appreciate the offer but I'm perfectly capable of buying my own drinks."

She paused for a moment, looking at him and Lucas was sure he saw a flash of interest in her green eyes. "I'm also not interested in company so, if you don't mind?"

"Sure" he said with a small smile. "I'm not looking for company either, just thought you looked like you had a tough day, that's all."

Her cool gaze swept over him and to his astonishment, he felt a shiver of excitement running through him. Damn if he wasn't attracted to her stand-offish attitude!

"Why would you care?"

Her question took him by surprise and he had to get his thoughts back on track before replying.

"I guess because I had the day from hell, so when I saw you knocking back your drinks, I figured yours hadn't gone too well either."

That brought a small smile to her lips.

"Okay, one drink, nothing else."

It was a clear statement, delivered in a cool tone and Lucas wasn't going to argue. He ordered another Scotch for her and beer for himself.

He held out his hand. "I'm Lucas, by the way."

She placed her small hand into his, her grip firm.

"Sabrina"

"Nice to meet you Sabrina." He watched in alarm as her green eyes widened with a look of pure panic. For a second, he thought he'd imagined it because just as quickly, she schooled her features. Withdrawing her hand to pick up her drink, he saw that her other hand was wrapped around the brass rail running the full length of the bar in a white-knuckle grip and wondered what the hell had just happened.

Chapter 7

Pacing her apartment in nervous agitation, Sabrina wondered where her cool and collected persona had disappeared to. Going away for a few days was supposed to be relaxing, instead she felt more tightly strung now than when she'd left. Instead of catching up on rest, the old nightmares had come back to haunt her with a vengeance, leaving her exhausted. She'd resorted to taking a Valium just so she could get a few hours sleep without waking up in a cold sweat, shivering with fear. Cutting short her vacation, she'd returned home and for the first time in a very long time, she was unsure of what to do next. No, that wasn't true. She knew what she needed to do but the fear she'd pushed away successfully for many years had taken hold again and she didn't know how to shake it off. Memories of her first year alone threatened to overwhelm her. Sabrina had spent that year in haze of drugs and alcohol, needing the calm the medication and booze gave her just to survive. She'd slowly managed to wean herself off them and had found that the only way to hold the nightmares at bay was by refusing to remember. Her need to survive was paramount, so pushing everything into the furthest recesses of her mind, she gradually managed to make a life for herself, a life where fear and loneliness had no place. Focusing solely on her assignments gave her the strength to do what she did, thoughts of the past firmly locked away. Now though, that no longer seemed possible. Seeing the pictures of the Senator, grinning at her from the glossy pages, she felt as if he knew that she was still out there, cowering in fear and that really pissed her off! So, she would focus on that anger and get the bastard. She would have to use all of her cunning and expertise, planning everything right down to the last tiny detail to ensure that this time, she would win. It would be her walking away with a distasteful look on her face as he lay there, slowly bleeding to death. Taking a deep breath, Sabrina got to work, spending long hours on the net, searching for every bit of information she could dig up. And there was a lot. He'd been a Senator for almost ten years and during that time, he'd made thousands of headlines, mostly because of his ultra conservative views. Anything from condemning abortion to gay rights and his misogynist views of the role of women in general, she was repulsed by everything he stood for. She really would be doing the world a favour by putting an end to this miserable son of a bitch! Startled by the thought, she leaned back in her chair. Is that what she had been doing? Thinking her assignments were for the greater good? Or was it just that she too was rotten to the core, so completely fucked that what she did seemed okay? Refusing to think about the state of her sanity, she moved back to her screen and typed a message to one of her contacts. None of the people she dealt with online knew the real her, nor did she know who they were but that wasn't important. Over the years, she had built up a small network of contacts who could get her what she needed, no questions asked. She didn't care how her requests where met, she paid handsomely and on time, so it worked both ways. As far as she knew, none of her contacts knew of the others, she made sure to keep her identity concealed as much as possible. Even her go to guy for fake identities didn't know exactly what she looked like; she changed her appearance for every assignment, the only certain fact he knew was that she was a female. Sabrina always did the ground work herself, setting up a new person, getting the appropriate details to ensure her new ID would hold up. Her contact would then deliver the papers a few days later. It was that simple. Typing out the message, she requested information on the private life of a particular Senator and by that, it was understood without having to be said, the seedier, predatory life of a monster. She knew with absolute certainty that there would be some information she could use in order to dole out the justice he so richly deserved. Once the request had been sent, she got up and, as she always did when she started a new assignment, went shopping to get her new persona set up.

Several hours later, she was back at her apartment, loaded up with bags of designer clothes, hair dye and other assorted items she needed to assume her new identity. Since she'd already decided on a name, all she had to do was send a photo to complete her new papers. They would be ready in the next few days. The 'new' her was a complete fabrication, not like Evie. She didn't need as much background for her next assignment as she had with the previous one. This one would be shorter, a superficial history of her 'past life' would suffice. She would take on the role of a wealthy socialite, albeit an educated one since Sabrina couldn't bear to even play-act at being dumb, who was looking to get involved in politics. A young woman who felt the need to prove that she could stand on her own two feet. The new her was bored with high society parties and meeting with other like- minded women who depended entirely on either a super-rich Daddy or an equally rich husband to fund their lifestyle. When she checked her messages a little while later, she saw that her contact had acknowledged her request with a promise to get back to her as soon as he'd found what she needed.

***

A few days later, she dressed in one of her new designer suits, did her make-up, put on expensive looking jewellery and got ready for a trip to DC. Scoping out an opportunity to find out the Senators' schedule, she figured the best place to start would be with a trip to Capitol Hill. She'd made an initial contact with his press office, enquiring about any possibilities of supporting the Senator in his work. Gushing about the bastard had been difficult but she'd pulled it off. The woman at the other end of the phone had been delighted to hear that Sabrina wanted to play a part and when she'd told the woman that she would be quite pleased to provide financial support, if needed, it was pretty much a done deal that at some point, she would get an invite to meet the man in person. So, for today, she was going on a fact-finding mission. She needed to check out the apartment he stayed at during the week. His main residence was the same house she'd moved into as a young girl, a house of horrors in more ways than one. It was in that house that her mother had begun her downward spiral, ending in her death. The same house where Sabrina herself had endured years of neglect, culminating in THAT night. Finding out about access to his apartment and how easy it would be to get him alone was crucial since she would have to find a way to get into the building without anyone paying undue attention to her. She'd found his address easily enough and was now sitting in her car parked a few yards away from the entrance, keeping an eye on the comings and goings. Security didn't seem particularly tight although you never knew. Someone as important as a Senator would have added security and she needed to know what exactly the set up was. Once she had the address, it was easy to find the name of the realtor who dealt in leasing the apartments within the building and, as luck would have it, one was currently vacant. She'd set up a viewing for today and had stressed the need for security without giving any real reasons as to why this would be important to her. The realtor arrived on time and escorted Sabrina into the foyer. She wasn't surprised by the opulence that greeted her; the marble floors, discreetly placed massive planters and a concierge in livery, it all smacked of sophistication and an almost limitless budget. Getting into the elevator, she saw immediately that renting an apartment wouldn't help her get to her target. The top floor was only accessible with a special key and Sabrina was sure that the Senator's apartment was up there. Feigning interest for half an hour as the realtor gushed about the place and its views of Capitol Hill and the White House, Sabrina smiled and nodded in all the right places but her mind was already occupied with another way to get to the Senator. Promising to let him have her decision within a couple of days, she took off, heading back to Baltimore, determined to find a way to carry out what would be her last assignment. Feeling frustrated and unwilling to go back home just yet, she decided to stop for a drink at a hotel near her apartment. She needed to regroup and figure out how the hell she was going to get close enough to kill the Senator.

When the man at the bar spoke to her, she was irritated at having her train of thought interrupted by some guy looking for a hook up. Despite that irritation, she found herself studying the man, feeling strangely drawn to him, a feeling she didn't know what to do with. He was a little older than her, his dark hair just a little too long but he had an attractive face with gorgeous hazel eyes. She couldn't tell how tall he was since he was sat on the bar stool but judging by the length of his legs, casually stretched out in front of him, he was well over six feet. When he gave her his line about having had a bad day at the office, she relented. Against her better judgment, she accepted his offer of a drink and when he introduced himself, she nearly fainted when she realised what she'd said. No one in the past ten years had called her Sabrina, a name she'd never used since the day she crept out of the house in the middle of the night. It took all her strength to hang on to the rail at the bar to stop herself from collapsing at the shock of hearing her given name.

Chapter 8

Lucas watched the woman in front of him and on instinct wanted to put a hand out to keep her steady. Something on her face told him that if he were to touch her, she'd bolt and that was the last thing he wanted to happen. So instead, he grabbed the nearest bar stool, pushing it next to his.

"Why don't you have a seat? You look like you could do with it."

He kept his voice low and calm and was rewarded with a nod and a whispered thank you as she sank gratefully into the seat. He waited patiently as she gathered herself, hoping she would offer some sort of explanation but she just sat there, staring at the drink before her. He watched as she took a deep breath, straightened her shoulders and then turned to him with a smile on her face, a smile that didn't quite reach her beautiful green eyes.

"Sorry about that!" She said with a little laugh and pointed to the glass in her hand. "I guess I shouldn't have had two of these on an empty stomach."

Lucas smiled but he didn't think for a minute that her excuse was true. Something was going on with her, of that he was sure. He was good at reading people, he had to be, doing the job he did. But for now, he planned to go along with her, sure that sooner or later, he'd get the real reason for her strange reaction out of her. He took his seat next to her and nodded.

"Yeah, not always a good idea. Listen, I know what you said earlier about not wanting company but how about we have something to eat? You know, to line our stomachs a little?" He gave her a grin and waited.

Her green eyes scanned his face as if trying to see if he had an ulterior motive by asking her to eat with him. Her scrutiny was slightly odd but he kept his calm and just waited for her to speak. He could see in her eyes that she was having a debate with herself whether or not to accept his invitation. He hoped she would.

"Why? I mean, apart from the fact that a little food helps absorb the booze. Why are you asking me?"

Okay, not what he had expected but he could deal.

"Why? Well I haven't eaten since this morning. So there is that. But also, I think I would enjoy having some company since I usually eat on my own unless I manage to talk my buddy into having a pizza with me. Not to mention you're way better looking than him."

He added the last bit in the hope of making her smile and sure enough, the corners of her lush mouth turned up. Lucas let out a breath he hadn't realised he'd been holding.

"I guess that works" she said, still smiling. "Where do you want to eat?"

"We can eat here or go elsewhere. Up to you."

Chapter 9

Sabrina wasn't used to having to decide for anyone other than herself. Should she really be doing this? She couldn't deny the fact that she felt drawn to him, he was, after all, a good-looking man but never having felt such a strong pull towards a member of the opposite sex was disconcerting, to say the least. She should be concentrating at finding a way to get to the Senator, not having dinner with a man she just met. Although, he was attractive, she admitted to herself. He was tall and well built, not in a muscle head kind of way but he seemed to keep himself fit. The suit he wore fitted well across his broad shoulders, his hazel eyes looking at her with friendly interest. Deciding to throw caution to the wind, because after all, she did need to eat, she nodded.

"Why don't we stay here. I've heard the restaurant is quite good."

He may be attractive but she wasn't about to go anywhere with him. At least here, she was close to home, should she need to escape.

Lucas stood, a grin on his face as he drained the last of his beer.

"Great! Let's see if they have a table available."

He stood to one side but made no attempt at touching her to help her off her bar stool. Sabrina wasn't sure whether she was pleased about that or not. Over the years, she'd made an effort to try and have some connection with the rest of humanity. At the beginning, she'd kept away from bars, just the thought of sleeping with a man making her break out in a cold sweat. Then she'd come across a leaflet from a local dog shelter looking for volunteer helpers and she had decided there and then, she would go and see what she could do to help. As a young girl, she'd had a little dog, not a pure race but a street mix, who followed her wherever she went like a little shadow. When her mother had married Steven and his campaign to become

Senator was well under way, he'd decided that her beloved pet didn't fit the picture he wanted to portray as a Senate candidate. So, he'd gotten rid of it. Sabrina would never forget the day she came home from school and finding Mikey had been taken to the vets and put to sleep.

Her mother was waiting for her that day and Sabrina knew straight away that something was wrong. At this stage, her mother still occasionally showed traces of her sweet Mama. She stood there, her eyes glittering with unshed tears.

"What's the matter?" Sabrina asked, beginning to feel a little scared. Her mother put a hand out to her and pulled her close.

"I don't know how to tell you, sweetie, but Mikey has passed away. I'm so sorry!"

Sabrina stood there, shaking her head, not able to make any sense of what her mother was saying.

"What do you mean? He was fine this morning!" Her voice getting louder with her distress, Sabrina felt tears welling up. Before her mother could reply, Steven came out of his office.

"Stop with the snivelling!" He said, his voice cold and loud. "I've told you before, Sabrina, in my line of work, image is important. The dog was the ugliest thing I've ever seen and I can't have the press office release pictures of us as a family with something as ugly as that. So we've had him put down. If you insist on having a dog, we'll get a Retriever or something."

Sabrina stared at him in shock at his callous words. Looking at her mother, who was wiping tears off her cheeks, leaving black streaks of Mascara on her face, she shook her head.

"You killed my dog?"

Steven sneered and shook his head. "Don't be so melodramatic, it was only a stupid dog."

"Steven, please ..." Her mother tried to intervene but he turned on her, grabbing her arm roughly.

"Enough, Serena! I've told you more than once you pander far too much to your daughter's silly notions. I've made a decision, since you seem unable to so yourself and she'll get used to it. I don't want to hear anymore about it." He viewed Sabrina and her mother with a look of disgust. "And get cleaned up, both of you. We are due for a photo session in half an hour so you better be presentable." With that, he turned and marched back into his office.

Her mother had tried to console her but the harsh words from Steven, telling her to stop being a snivelling brat had sown the seeds of hate, a hate that had grown with each passing month.

Chapter 10

The decision to help out at the dog shelter had saved her in more ways than she realised. The unconditional love the dogs showed her made it possible for her to engage with the other volunteers, although she kept a certain distance nonetheless. Every time she relocated, she would find another shelter and her services were always accepted gratefully. The first time she'd attempted at getting to know a man had been with another volunteer. Logan had been easy going, so Sabrina had decided to test the waters and had gone on a date with him. When he kissed her before saying goodbye, she'd felt nothing which was not unexpected. She hadn't been sure about going out with him in the first place. Telling him the next time she saw him that she didn't want to pursue anything with him, he'd smiled and shrugged his shoulders. It would be another six months and in a different state before Sabrina met Paul, a guy who hade made her want to try again, her body's natural responses kicking in and when she slept with him, it hadn't been disastrous. She'd felt fine although he couldn't evoke more than mild pleasure during sex. Since then, she'd only met one other man who stirred her and that man was currently standing beside her. Lucas seemed to affect her more than anyone else and Sabrina didn't know how she felt about that. When she'd shaken his hand, just before she'd blurted out her real name to him, she'd felt a connection, something she'd never experienced before. Even though she didn't know anything about Lucas, he didn't make her feel threatened. His friendly demeanour seemed to have a calming effect on her rattled nerves.

"You're awfully quiet there. Are you having second thoughts?"

His voice held a hint of a smile and Sabrina couldn't help the small smile appearing on her face.

"Sorry! I'm fine, thank you. Just a little tired I guess."

The appearance of a waiter prevented further talking and Sabrina watched as Lucas spoke with quiet authority, the waiter smiling and nodding at his request for a table. He led the way into the restaurant and brought them to a table by one of the windows, pulling out a chair for Sabrina. Once seated, he handed them a menu, asked if they wanted an aperitif and then left them to make their choice when they declined. Pretending to read the menu, Sabrina cast a glance at Lucas only to find him watching her. Embarrassed at being caught staring, she dived behind the menu and heard him chuckle softly. Putting the menu down, she raised her eyes to his and couldn't help but return his smile.

"Have you decided on something?"

She'd expected some comment about having caught her looking at him and was surprised to find herself relax.

"I'll have the seabass" she said. "What about you?"

"Hmm … I'm not a great lover of fish so I think I'll go with the braised beef."

Just then, the waiter reappeared, bringing a carafe of water along with a small basket of freshly baked rolls.

"Have you decided on your order?" He smiled at Sabrina, pen at the ready.

"Would you like some wine with your dinner?" He asked after writing down their choices.

Lucas raised a questioning brow but Sabrina shook her head. She'd had enough alcohol for one night.

"I think I'll pass but you go ahead."

"Just a beer for me then, thank you."

Nodding, the waiter collected the menu cards and disappeared to place their order.

"Can I ask what you do for a living?" Lucas said smiling.

"Well, I'm between jobs at the moment" she replied after just a moment of hesitation. Seeing that Lucas was waiting for her to continue, she decided to go with a partial truth.

"I'm trying to get a job in DC. That's where I was today."

"Are you looking for anything in particular?" Lucas sounded genuinely interested.

"I'm hoping to work in Politics, not sure what yet. I've spoken to several Senator's offices to see what's available." Sabrina paused. She felt uncomfortable about giving too much information about herself. It wasn't something she ever did so she decided to turn the conversation back to him.

"What about you?"

Lucas looked at her for a brief moment, as if he wasn't sure what to tell her.

"I work for the FBI."

He said at last and it took all of Sabrina's willpower not to react to his words. Keeping her face as straight as she could, she managed to muster what she hoped was a realistic smile.

"That sounds interesting" she said, amazed at how calm her voice sounded.

"It has its moments." Lucas said with a grin.

Sabrina let out a quiet sigh of relief. He hadn't noticed her reaction and for that she was glad but at the same time, she realised that she would not be seeing Lucas again after tonight. She could not afford to get involved with an FBI agent. Her thoughts brought a pang of regret, something she would never have imagined happening. He seemed like a nice guy and, if circumstances had been different, maybe she could have gotten to know him a little better. Sabrina shook her head at her silly musings, she'd chosen a path for herself and if Lucas were to have any inkling who she really was, he would come after her with all the might of the FBI. Unwilling to carry on with this particular train of thoughts, she forced herself to refocus on the conversation.

"Can you tell me a little more about what you do or is it need to know only?"

He laughed at that and shook his head. "I'm with the FBI not the CIA, sweetheart." He got serious as he continued.

"We're in the middle of a murder investigation, so it's hectic at the moment."

Sabrina felt a shudder running down her spine, wondering if Lucas was referring to her last assignment. If he was, she didn't want to know but before she could change the subject, he carried on.

"I'm sure you've must have seen it on the news? This latest murder is thought to be linked to five other murders, so we're talking serial killer."

"Good grief! Of course!"

She hadn't seen the news, she never watched them. She didn't even own a TV but she couldn't very well tell him that without sounding odd. Lucas must have seen something of her disquiet because he gave her a reassuring smile.

"Anyway, I think we can find nicer things to talk about than murder, don't you?"

She was saved from answering as the waiter approached with their meals. Her appetite ruined by the rising panic that threatened to take her breath away, she picked at her food, a fact that didn't escape Lucas's notice.

"Is something wrong with your food?"

Sabrina shook her head. "No, but I'm not feeling well. I sometimes get migraines and I think tonight is one of those times."

She put down her knife and fork, noticing her hands shaking as the urge to run suddenly overwhelmed her. Fishing her wallet out of her bag, she withdrew some cash and laid it in front of Lucas.

"I'm so sorry, but I need to get home before it gets any worse." She got up and picked up her jacket.

"It was nice meeting you, Lucas."

Without waiting for his reply, she walked out of the restaurant as fast as she could, glad she wasn't wearing heels. Once outside the hotel, she broke into a run as if the devil himself was after her and didn't stop until she reached her building. She knew only too well that the devil was waiting for her in Washington.

Chapter 11

With more work than you could shake a stick at, Lucas often worked ten-hour days. Just because they hadn't gotten anywhere with the X murder case didn't mean that some other stupid fuckers had stopped going around killing, thus making sure the Baltimore FBI office was kept busy. Five weeks had passed since the murder of victim number six and both he and Dan had been assigned to other cases. Logically, he understood that there was no point going over the same files day after day but he was still convinced that they had missed an important clue. Though what the hell that was, he didn't know. Besides that, his thoughts often went back to the night he'd met Sabrina. Her sudden flight from the restaurant bothered him. He hadn't believed her excuse about having a migraine, not for one damn minute. Something had happened to make her take off the way she did but for the life of him, he couldn't figure out what had triggered such severe panic. Because that was what had happened to her. He'd seen it in her eyes, the way her breath was coming in short bursts as if she'd just finished a fast sprint. All these signs told him that something had spooked her to such an extent that she ran off as if her life depended on it. Shaking his head, he forced himself to refocus on his work. There was no point wondering what had happened, she was gone and he didn't think he'd see her again. He was just about ready to call it day when his phone rang.

"Lucas?"

The voice at the other end was quiet, almost a whisper but he recognised it instantly.

"Sabrina, is that you?"

Of all the people, she was the last one he'd expected to hear from. For a split second, he thought she'd hung up but then he heard her let out a quiet sigh and his senses went on high alert.

"It is, yes."

More silence and Lucas had to stop himself from bombarding her with questions. He knew without a shadow of a doubt that she'd thought long and hard about calling him and he wasn't going to do anything that would make her disappear again.

"How are you?" He kept his voice calm, holding his breath.

"Okay, I guess." Her voice was louder now, more confident. "I wanted to apologise for running out on you that night."

He took a quiet breath before answering.

"Hey, it's okay."

He wanted to tell her that he'd thought about her often, that he couldn't get her out of his mind but that wasn't going to work, so he kept silent.

"Thank you." She said and he could hear the relief in her voice that he hadn't been mad at her for taking off.

"Anyway, I was thinking, if you want, maybe we could go for dinner or something? When you have time that is?"

"I'd love to" he replied immediately, surprised to find that he really did. "Are you still in Baltimore?"

"No, I mean yes!" She let out an embarrassed laugh.

"Let me say this right. I'm leaving for DC tomorrow and thought before I go, I could to make it up to you, you know?"

Lucas had to smile at her obvious uncertainty.

"Tonight would be good, in fact I was just about to leave work. You caught me just on my way out."

"Are you sure? I mean, if you have plans already …"

"I don't and I would love to go to dinner with you, okay?" He cut in, not wanting her to doubt his willingness to meet. "Where did you have in mind?"

He was surprised when she mentioned the name of a small Italian place not too far from where he lived. He'd been there several times before and knew the food was good.

"That's quite a coincidence" he said with a laugh.

"Oh? Why is that?"

"It's not far from where I live so I'll get a chance to go home and change. What time were you thinking?"

Arranging to meet her at the restaurant for eight, she'd refused his offer to come and collect her from her place, he made his way home, wondering why she'd waited so long to get in touch. He had a feeling that the beautiful Sabrina hadn't always been treated kindly by members of his own sex. He could hear it in the uncertain and hesitant way she had spoken and his heart went out to her. He bet anything she didn't realise just what a beauty she was. Someone had to have been responsible for her to act the way she did. As he showered, he wondered if he was ever going to find out.

Chapter 12

The day after her disastrous encounter with Lucas, Sabrina packed up her old life. Apart from a couple of suitcases of clothes and of course, her precious computer, she owned very little. The apartment had come fully furnished and as she picked up the last of her things, she didn't look back over the space she'd called home for over six months. This had been Evie's place and Evie no longer existed. She pulled the door closed behind her, took the elevator down to the underground parking and stowed her belongings in her car. She hadn't yet made arrangements for a new place in DC but she wasn't worried about that. She had a few weeks to get set up, the Senator would be on honeymoon for a week after the wedding. Reassuring herself she had time to put her plan into action, finding somewhere to live was the least of her problems. When you had money, renting at short notice was never an issue. She'd booked herself into one of the many hotels in DC, taking full advantage of the excellent room service while she got settled. After making a few enquiries, she'd signed a six-month lease for a fully furnished cute little house in a quiet neighbourhood and had moved in two days later. The owners were overseas, apparently the husband had some work thing that meant staying away for a minimum of six to nine months. It was perfect for her. Now she could begin to set up an exact plan on how she was going to achieve her goal. She had received her new identity as requested, she was now Katie Palmer, a graduate from MIT with a degree in political science, looking for a foothold in the Capitol. Her papers were excellent as always and she'd set up a full background history for Katie, should anyone feel the need to check. Sabrina assumed that, if she managed to get a job in the Senators' office, a background check was inevitable, so she made sure it all stacked up. She'd included a list of fake hobbies, portraying herself as wealthy trust fund baby, bored with her current life style and wanting a new challenge. Printing her fake CV, she made an appointment at the Senators' office to be interviewed by someone called

Sonia Whitmore. The position she was applying for was for a lowly office worker, no benefits for the first six months and lousy pay but it was a way to get access and that was all that mattered.

On the day of the interview, she dressed with care, the expensive suit elegant but very simple. She put her dark brown hair into a loose bun and slipped on the thick rimmed fake glasses. Sabrina's vision was excellent but she figured that some one as studious and intelligent as Katie would wear glasses. Besides, it helped at disguising her facial features, just in case she came across the Senator by chance.

Her interview went well, Sonia was impressed by her credentials but even more so when Katie mentioned that her father had made contributions to every campaign the Senator had fought. Sonia was very pleased indeed and had offered her the job on the spot, telling Sabrina she could start the following Monday. Sonia prepared an employee ID, a laminated card attached to a red ribbon and handed it to her.

"This will get you into the building Monday morning. Please make sure you have it on you at all times."

Sonia explained the swiping-in process to gain access to the offices, pointing at the bar code at the back of the card.

"For now, you'll have only limited access to certain areas of the suite of offices, but I'm sure you'll move up quickly. You seem like a very intelligent young woman and hard work as well as good time keeping will help that process." Sonia said with an encouraging smile.

Sabrina nodded in agreement. No, it wouldn't take long at all. In fact, Sonia had no clue just how quickly Sabrina would gain access. Once in the job, she knew hacking into the system to up her security clearance would pose no problem.

"I'll give you a quick tour if you like, I think the Senator is in today. Would you like to meet him?"

She looked at Sabrina as if she'd just told her she'd won the lottery. The hell she did! Putting a very convincing sad look on her face, she wrung her hands.

"Oh, I would love that but I have to go and see my Grandma at the hospital. I had a call this morning to say that she wasn't going to last much longer."

Pausing for effect, she watched as Sonia's pudgy face fell.

"Oh dear! I'm real sorry to hear that. Of course, you must go. I'll show you around next week when you start."

***

With a few days free before she was starting her new job, Sabrina spent the next day searching out the nearest shelter to her current home and made a phone call to enquire about volunteer work.

"That would be just great, Katie."

The young woman on the other end said enthusiastically. She'd introduced herself as Jenny and was only too pleased when Sabrina offered to come by the next day.

"I must warn you though" she said with a laugh. "If you get here early, you'll be shovelling poop for a while!"

Laughing, Sabrina assured Jenny that it wouldn't be an issue, telling her about her previous volunteer work.

"Great! I look forward to meeting you tomorrow."

As always when she entered a busy shelter, Sabrina's heart warmed at the sight of all the different dogs, barking excitedly as she was shown around by Jenny the next day.

"We currently have twenty dogs looking for a forever home." Jenny explained as she showed her where supplies and cleaning materials were kept.

"We do not destroy dogs, ever!" Sabrina nodded, pleased at the vehemence in Jenny's voice.

"I'm glad to hear that." She said with a smile.

"Now tell me what you want me to do. I'm ready for some serious poop shovelling."

Jenny laughed and handed her a shovel, small dustpan and a large container.

"There you go. You can start with Satan!"

Watching her face, Jenny couldn't hold back her laughter.

"Don't worry, he's a sweetie, really. Come on, I'll introduce you."

Sabrina followed a still laughing Jenny to one of the kennels where a tiny Chihuahua was barking excitedly at their approach.

"Hey boy! You've got a new friend today!" Jenny said to the dog as she opened the pen.

Before Sabrina knew what was happening, the little dog leapt up, trying to lick her hands, barking madly. Bending down, she let him sniff her hand before his pink tongue gave her a thorough licking. Looking up at Jenny, Sabrina smiled.

"Satan?"

"Yeah, I know!" Jenny giggled. "His previous owner, one of our volunteers, had a weird sense of humour but Daniel loved the little tinker more than life itself."

Her voice grew quiet. "Sadly, he passed away two months ago so this little guy ended up here."

Sabrina bent down to stroke the little dog again.

"I'm sorry to hear that. Let's hope someone will find you soon, little one."

Straightening up, she turned to Jenny. "Right, I'll get started then, yeah?"

An hour later, the kennels were cleaned and Sabrina had been introduced to two other volunteers, both students who loved dogs and had some spare time to help. Annie was a tall, leggy blonde while Aisha was a short and very well rounded Hispanic girl. Their unlikely friendship made Sabrina smile. The girls had told her that they had met on the very first day at College, having been assigned to the same dorm. Despite their different backgrounds, they had become instant friends and did most things together. Even picking up guys, Annie informed her with a saucy wink.

"You'll have to come with us one of these days, Katie" she said.

"Aisha is a master at picking the fittest, best looking guys around. I always compere her to a honey pot; the bees can't help themselves!"

Laughing at her droll words, Sabrina thanked them for the offer and said she'd be sure to do just that. She had no intention of taking up their invitation, her attention had to focus solely on her assignment. For now, at least, she couldn't afford any distraction. And just like that, her mind conjured up a picture of a certain tall, dark haired man who'd been on her mind far too often for her liking. In her own way, she had mourned the fact that she'd never see him again, but the risk was simply too great. And yet, sometimes, just before she went to sleep, his image would appear in her minds' eye, making her wonder whether he ever thought about her. She thought it unlikely, her odd behaviour that night would have seen to it that he'd thought himself better off without her. And that made her surprisingly sad.

Chapter 13

Sabrina spent the first week in her new job bored out of her mind. After having been given "The Tour" by Sonia, thankfully the Senator wasn't in, she'd been shown to her desk and was given a large folder with fundraising details which needed transferring onto the system. By Wednesday she was at breaking point and decided to have a little fun. She fed an error code into the system, making the entire program go haywire. Enjoying the resulting chaos, because anything was better than the tedious work she was forced to do, she kept her head down as Darren, the IT guy, came and took over her seat, trying to restore order. Her keen mind processed his keystrokes, storing the information for later use. He really was an idiot, typing in access codes in front of her without hesitation. Then it took him a good half hour to find the problem. Another twenty minutes later, he'd restored her work. With a huff he told her to be more careful and then left without another word. Sabrina was beyond surprised that he hadn't realised that the fault couldn't have produced itself. Apparently, the guy had thought that something she'd done accidentally had made the system crash. In a way she had but not by accident. Mentally shrugging her shoulders, she figured that with such an idiot in charge, the security wasn't going to pose any problems for her later.

"Jeez, he's grumpy!" She said to Sonia who had fretted the whole time.

"It's not like I did it on purpose!"

She worked hard at keeping a straight face as Sonia heaved a sigh.

"Yes, well, he has a lot on his plate at the moment."

That comment picked Sabrina's curiosity.

"Why? Is there a problem with the system?"

Sonia shook her head. "No, but with the Senator's forthcoming marriage, there are a lot of temps working here, to help the Press office dealing with the event. Often these young girls don't know much about computers and he's been run off his feet trying to sort out their mess, poor thing."

It dawned on Sabrina that Sonia was sweet on the guy, judging from the way she'd hovered over him, offering him coffee and even some snacks while he'd worked at Sabrina's desk. It was blindingly obvious to anyone with a pair of eyes, apart from Sonia apparently, that the poor woman was on a hide to nowhere. He'd flat out refused any of her offerings, grumbling something about not having time for a tea party. Stupid jerk! Sonia was better off without him but she wasn't going to point that out to her. Instead, she apologised for having created such havoc and then got on with her job.

Since she'd made sure she worked as slowly as she could possibly get away with, by the time five o'clock came around, she hadn't finished her work. Sonia had an appointment which meant she had to leave on time and at first, was reluctant to leave her alone to finish but Sabrina assured her she'd be fine.

"If I don't catch up, I'll be snowed under tomorrow." She said, hoping the woman would take the hint and leave.

"I wouldn't want to fall behind in my first week." She added for good measure.

Obviously pleased by her eagerness to do a good job, Sonia finally agreed and left. Sabrina waited a good ten minutes to make sure she wasn't coming back and then went and sat at Sonia's computer and got to work. Since the IT guy had inadvertently revealed his master access code whilst working on her computer, she'd had no problem getting in and accessing the necessary program although she'd have gotten in even without the codes. Just as she had suspected, the security was laughable and Sabrina wondered how that guy managed to keep his job. Ten minutes later, she had what she'd been looking for. The program in front of her allowed the person with the appropriate access to increase the security levels of employees. It also detailed the varying levels of approved security for the current staff. Seeing as Sonia had clearance to all levels, she simply printed off another employee ID card in Sonia's name. If anyone bothered to check, which she doubted that they would, given the lax approach by the IT guy, her own access level would appear untouched. Happy with her achievement, she closed down the program and then made sure to erase all traces of her work from Sonia's computer. She didn't think Darren was smart enough to work out what she'd done but she didn't believe in taking unnecessary risks. Step one of her plan was now achieved. She needed to set up a time table for her final encounter with the Senator, working out the best way to get him alone would require careful planning. Nothing could be allowed to go wrong so she would put everything into the assignment to ensure nothing would.

By Friday lunchtime, it all became too much. If she heard just one more comment about how wonderful the Senator was and how kind he was to invite all of his staff to come to the ceremony, she was going to scream. It seemed odd that nobody thought about the fact that they hadn't been invited for the reception afterwards, him being such a good guy and all. The excited staffers were talking about tomorrow's nuptials as if it were a royal occasion and Sabrina couldn't take anymore. She needed out of this office and pronto. Pretending to receive a call, she summoned her considerable acting skills and, after putting down the receiver on her phone, she turned to Sonia with a look of utter desolation on her face, even managing to make her eyes glisten with unshed tears.

"Oh goodness me! Whatever is the matter, Katie?" Sonia looked at her stricken face, getting up from her seat and walking towards Sabrina.

"Oh Sonia! That was the hospital! My Gran …" She didn't need to finish her sentence before she felt herself engulfed in Sonia's ample bosom.

"Oh, you poor thing! I'm so sorry, sweetie."

Sabrina mumbled something and tried to get out of the hold that was slowly suffocating her. Sonia released her, looking at her with pity.

"I'm sorry but would it be okay if I left early?" Sabrina let a couple of tears fall from her face and Sonia rushed to get her a tissue.

"Of course, dear." Handing her the tissue, she patted Sabrina's shoulder. "Don't you worry about anything. You go and say good bye."

Sabrina dabbed her eyes without taking off her glasses.

"Thank you so much. I'm sorry but I don't think I'll be at the ceremony tomorrow."

"I understand completely. It wouldn't exactly be appropriate. You just go and do what you need to do."

Thanking her profusely, Sabrina gathered her things and hightailed it out of the office. Half an hour later, she was pacing her living room floor, feeling like a trapped animal. She still hadn't come across anything that would help her get the Senator alone and it was driving her nuts. Usually, she didn't mind taking her time when working on a plan of action, but this one not only made her nervous, she also had a daily fight with herself, tamping down the fear that tried to raise its ugly head with predictable regularity. She couldn't afford to let that happen! When you were afraid, your instincts kicked in and the urge to take flight would be hard to fight! On a whim, Sabrina decided to go and visit the shelter. Spending a few hours in the company of friendly animals would help restore her rattled nerves. This time however, her canine therapy didn't seem to work, her mind whirling like a fairground merry-go-round. Thoughts of her plan and how she was going to achieve her goal were chased by images of Lucas, his warm smile making her aware just what she'd been missing out on over the years. Memories of her crappy teenage years threatened to resurface, intermingling with more recent events. Random images from her previous assignments kept creeping into her mind until she felt like screaming. Making her excuses just an hour later, she fled from the shelter, confused and upset, wondering how on earth she was going to face her Nemesis if she was already this close to breaking point. Once home, she did the only thing she could think of and took a Valium, hoping it would calm the demons, enabling her to clear her mind and get back on track. But even after the pill took effect and she felt calmer, Lucas's smiling face kept floating in front of her closed eyes, teasing her with what ifs. When she woke up a couple of hours later, she felt a lot calmer, her mind clear again and focused on what lay ahead. And then she did something she'd never thought she'd do. Grabbing her laptop, she opened a browser, and found the information she was looking for a short while later. She picked up the phone and dialled, not giving herself a chance to second guess her actions.

Chapter 14

Lucas arrived at the restaurant shortly before eight and found a convenient parking spot just a few steps away. Switching off the engine, he looked out the car window and saw that Sabrina was already there, waiting for him outside. He watched her for a few moments. She'd dressed in tight dark jeans, paired with what looked like biker boots and a leather jacket. A long woolly scarf was wrapped around her neck to protect her from the late November cold. She was pacing up and down, her head bent and even from his position, he could see that she was nervous. Pulling the keys from the ignition, he got out and made his way over to her, his heart suddenly beating faster. He watched in astonishment as her demeanour changed the minute she saw him approach. A big smile lit up her face, her eyes focused on him as he got closer.

"Lucas!"

He could hear the relief in her voice and wondered whether she'd thought he would stand her up. Closing the distance between them, he stood looking down into her brilliant green eyes, waiting, wanting to see what she would do next. Sabrina reached out and placed a gentle hand on his cheek, her eyes never leaving his.

"Hey."

Taking a deep breath, he put his large hand over hers and then brought her palm to his lips and kissed the soft skin there. Her sharp intake of breath told him that he wasn't the only one who felt the connection between them. When he'd first met her, it hadn't been anything sexual, just a feeling of wanting to get to know this woman but now, his spine tingled and he wanted to kiss her with an urgency he hadn't felt in a very long time. Her lips were close, her breath leaving small clouds of mist in the cold evening air and before he knew it, he put his mouth on hers. Just a touching of lips but even in its simplicity, the taste of her sent a sharp bolt of desire running through his system.

He felt her arms go around his neck as she closed the gap between them, her body pressed against his. When he felt her tongue sliding across his lips, Lucas pulled her into his arms and deepened the kiss with a groan. The kiss seemed to last forever and when he released his hold on her a little, he saw her green eyes holding his gaze with an intensity that fired his blood even more.

"I think we'd better get inside before we give the public a show."

He smiled, glad to see her grin back. He took her hand and opened the door to the restaurant for her. A young girl stood at the hostess counter and greeted them with a friendly smile.

"Good evening. Table for two?"

Picking up two menus, she led them through the half full restaurant towards a table at the back, waited until they were both seated and handed them the cards.

"Can I get you an aperitif while you choose?" The girl pulled out a notepad and pen.

"I'll have a glass of your house red, please" Sabrina smiled at the girl.

"How about we order a bottle?" Lucas looked at Sabrina. She nodded in agreement.

"Okay then, do you have any preference?"

"No, I'm not a great connoisseur of wine so you choose."

Lucas glanced at the wine list.

"A bottle of Barolo please."

Smiling, the girl noted his order and then left to fetch the wine.

"That was my Dads' favourite" he said. "He didn't drink it too often as it's quite pricey but when he did, he savoured every last drop."

"Do you still have your parents?" Sabrina asked.

"No, my Mom died from breast cancer when I was fourteen and Dad passed away a couple of years ago."

"I'm sorry." Sabrina reached over and placed a hand on his arm.

Lucas shrugged, not wanting to taint the atmosphere with sadness.

"They had me quite late in life. For a long time, they didn't think they could have children. What about you?"

"No, I have no family."

The finality in her tone told him not to probe any further. Lucas wondered again what had happened to her in the past to make her so closed off. After their kiss, Sabrina had seemed a lot more relaxed tonight, her face animated until he asked about family. His thoughts were interrupted by the arrival of the waitress, bringing the wine he'd ordered and Lucas was glad that this would give them the opportunity to get off an obviously painful subject. Filling their glasses, he raised his and smiled at Sabrina.

"Here's to a good evening."

Glad to see her smile making a comeback, he took a sip and then picked up the menu.

"I'll drink to that!" She followed suit and picked up her card, studied the available choice for a moment and then looked up.

"What are you having?"

"Oh, I know exactly what I'm ordering." He grinned at her. "I've eaten here before and since the very first time, I always have the shrimp ravioli for starters, followed by Osso Bucco and for dessert, the best Tiramisu in the whole of the US."

"Well now, I do like a man who knows what he wants!" Sabrina said with a straight face.

Lucas had to swallow hard as she winked at him, a laugh bubbling out of her, telling him she'd noticed his reaction. She was actually flirting with him? Damn, if that didn't make his mind stray in a totally inappropriate direction! Grinning, he raised his glass again.

"Glad to hear it."

Her eyes sparkled in the low light, all traces of their earlier conversation about non-existing family gone.

"What are you having?" He asked.

"I don't eat a lot of meat so I think I'll try the shrimp ravioli, but as a main. I'll have a salad to start and if I have any room left, I will certainly try this famous Tiramisu."

They passed their meal in light conversation, neither of them willing to spoil the warm atmosphere. Lucas couldn't remember that last time he'd enjoyed himself as much during a date. Sabrina was sparkling with wit and she had a wicked sense of humour as she regaled him with tales of her volunteer work at the dog shelter. Lucas had never had a dog but she sounded so animated, it was clear that she adored them.

"Sounds like you get a lot out of that." He said, enjoying her lively way of describing the antics of the animals.

"I do. I'll be sad not to go anymore." She gave a little sigh.

"Of course, you're moving to DC. Any luck with the job hunt?"

"Not yet." She shrugged her shoulders. "I've got several interviews lined up, one of them with a Senators' office, so, fingers crossed."

She didn't sound too down hearted about it. Lucas didn't really know anything about her background but he figured, someone was bound to give her an opportunity. She seemed determined enough.

"Have you found somewhere to live?"

Hesitating for just a second, Sabrina shook her head.

"I'm sharing with my friend Katie for now. DC is very expensive."

He could believe that. "So, I guess, getting a job is quite important?"

"It is." She smiled but said nothing more.

Lucas realised that she seemed reluctant to give too much away. She answered his questions with just enough information without adding any further detail. Another conundrum that made the woman sitting opposite him even more interesting.

Sharing a dessert, Sabrina insisted she couldn't manage a whole portion, he was delighted when she let him feed her, watching in fascination as her lips slid over the spoon, her pink tongue occasionally sneaking out to lick cream off the side of her mouth. His imagination ran wild thinking about her lips on a certain part of his anatomy and he had to shift a little in his seat to try and accommodate the growing tightness in his jeans. He didn't want presume anything but damn, he wanted to spend the night with her. His gaze met hers and what he saw in her beautiful green eyes gave him the courage to say what was on his mind.

"Fancy getting out of here?"

His tone left no doubt about the meaning of his words. Sabrina studied him for a moment, her gaze intent. Holding his breath, he waited for her reply.

"I thought you'd never ask!"

Her voice was soft but full of the same heat as his thoughts. After paying the bill, he put his hand on the small of her back, escorting her out of the restaurant. They stood facing each other, neither speaking with words but their eyes communicated their mutual desire to take the next step. Lucas cleared his throat and then took her hand, crossing the road to his car.

"Want to come back to my place?" His question hung in the cold night air.

"Yes, I would like that very much."

Her simple answer made his heart beat faster. Taking a deep breath, he nodded and opened the door for her, making sure she was buckled in before closing it softly. It wasn't far to get back to his place and neither of them spoke on the short drive. Lucas held her small hand in his larger one as he drove home, parking in front of his house and switching off the engine. He turned to look at her and found her gazing at him, the desire clearly written on her beautiful face.

"Are you sure?" Lucas asked.

Sabrina nodded. "I am, yes. You?"

Instead of answering, he placed a gentle hand on her neck and drew her to him, putting his lips on hers. Her instant response confirmed her words and sent a thrill of hot desire down his spine. He simultaneously wanted to spend the whole night just kissing her and get her into his bed at the same time. Reluctantly, he pulled away, stroking a hand down her soft cheek.

"Let's go before I forget we're in the car and get carried away!" He grinned at her, loving the fact that she laughed and then released her seat belt.

Pulling his keys out of his pocket, he grabbed her hand and led her to the door, unlocking it before stepping back to let her enter first. He switched on the hall light and then stood watching her, memorising the picture of her standing in his home. She stood straight, her eyes on him as if waiting to see what he'd do next. Lucas wanted to rush, strip her out of her clothes and ravish her against the door but that wouldn't do. He wanted to take his time with her, explore her and somehow, he knew instinctively that the only way with Sabrina was to go slow and be gentle.

"Let me take your coat." He said while slipping off his own.

"Would you like a drink?" He asked after taking her jacket.

Without answering, she turned to him, closing the gap between them and pressed her body against his. Her arms sneaked around his neck as Lucas stood perfectly still, hardly daring to breathe. Her mouth was hovering close to his own and then, with a sigh, she kissed him. It took all of his willpower to stop himself from devouring her, instead he let her settle the speed and intensity of the kiss.

"What I want" she said as they came up for air, "is for you to take me to bed."

Chapter 15

Lucas woke up with an unfamiliar weight across his chest. A shift in the weight made him open his eyes. His mind still fuzzy from sleep, he couldn't at first comprehend what he was looking at. Sabrina was straddling his chest, one arm raised above her head, the blade of a knife glinting in the early morning light. Frozen with shock, he looked up into her beautiful green eyes and didn't recognise the woman before him, her stare cold and almost inhuman. With a smile on her face, she brought down the blade and he felt the cold metal slip between his ribs and into his chest, piercing his heart.

With a muffled scream, Lucas woke up, sweat drenching his body as he realised he'd been dreaming. He grabbed the sheet that was tangled across his body and wiped his face, only then realising that he was alone in his bed. He reached over where Sabrina was supposed to be and found the sheets cold. He listened into the silence of his room and knew she'd gone. With a shudder, he tried to make sense of it all. His nightmare had been so real, he still felt the cold fear that had gripped him when she'd plunged the blade into his chest. He lay there for a moment longer, trying to get his mind into some sort of order. It was scary to think that his work was taking over his mind, manifesting itself in this ridiculous but extremely frightening nightmare. Lucas shook his head, trying to clear the image of the blade from his mind. He pulled his pillow up from behind his head and sat up, taking a deep breath. The horrible picture started to fade from his mind, instead he remembered when he'd woken the last time.

Sabrina was still beside him, laying on her side facing him. Her green gaze on his face, she'd smiled, reaching over and letting her fingers trace his cheek. He'd run his hands across her soft curves, enjoying the feel of her.

"Hey there, beautiful."

Without waiting for her response, he'd carried on with his exploration, trailing light kisses wherever he went. Her soft moans came slowly at first but when he reached the centre of her, she became more vocal, her hands tangling in his hair. Keeping up a steady rhythm, he drove her towards her climax until she crashed, her thighs holding him a willing prisoner. Rising up and nudging her legs apart further, he pushed into her wet heat and groaned. She fit him so perfectly, he had to keep himself still for a moment to savour the feeling of her soft inner walls hugging him, flexing around him as if to pull him in further. Placing his weight on his arms either side of her, he interlaced his hands with hers, kissing her with all he had. Moving at a slow steady pace, they came together and Lucas knew that, given time, he could fall for this woman like he'd never fallen before. Resting his forehead against hers as their breathing slowly returned to normal, he looked down at her, her beautiful green eyes glistening with unshed tears. Alarmed, he brought a hand to her face.

"What's the matter sweetheart? Did I hurt you?"

Feeling slightly panicked, he watched a single tear slide down her pale cheek. Sabrina wiped it away with a sad smile, shaking her head.

"Nothing's wrong." Reaching up to place a gentle hand on his cheek, she stared at him.

"I just didn't know it could be like this."

Her whispered words eased the panic in his chest. He hugged her to him, lost for words. He'd suspected that at some point in her life, something had happened to her. Now he wondered if she'd been raped or had suffered an attack of some kind. The sadness in her tone had touched him like nothing before and all he could think of doing right then was to hold her close. As her head settled on his chest, he kept one arm around her, his other hand gently stroking her until her even breathing told him that she'd fallen asleep. Lucas lay there for a long time, holding her, hoping that being in his arms would make her feel safe.

Apparently, it hadn't been enough. Checking his watch, he let out a sigh. He might as well get up, there was plenty of work waiting for him and going back to sleep was out of the question anyway. He showered and got dressed, making his way into the kitchen for a much-needed coffee when he saw the small piece of paper propped up against his coffee maker.

Thank you for giving me the best night of my life X

The note made him smile but then he realised, she hadn't left a number. The smile faded as he understood that he probably wasn't going to hear from her again and was surprised at the disappointment he felt. But he was being stupid. For a start, she was much younger than him and she was just starting a new chapter of her life in DC. Although it wasn't far, he knew that with his job and its unpredictable hours, a long-distance relationship wouldn't have worked anyway. Still, he couldn't seem to shake the feeling of wondering what if?

Chapter 16

Sabrina was back to pacing her living room floor. For the past two days, she'd locked herself away from the outside world. At war with herself, she couldn't believe what she'd done! Never in her life had she acted on instinct, and with good reason. What the hell had she been thinking, meeting up with Lucas again? Knowing that he could and would do everything to bring her to justice, if ever he found out who she really was. She hadn't realised until he'd told her that she'd been given a label by the press. The X murderer! Of course, that's what she was, a cold-blooded killer, there was no doubt about that. The fact that she only killed sick paedophiles who really didn't deserve to live didn't change anything. Murder was murder, at least in the eyes of the law, and Lucas was the law. When she'd phoned him, she hadn't thought about her assignments, all she'd felt was the need to see him one more time. She hadn't planned on sleeping with him but when he'd stood in front of her outside the restaurant, when he'd kissed her, she'd been lost. Lost in the feelings his kiss awakened, lost in possibilities of feeling like a normal person. She'd deluded herself to think she could ever be like any other woman, out on a date with a man. A man who knew how to make her world explode, making her want impossible things. She'd pushed away the thoughts that tried to invade her brain, the small voice inside telling her to be cautious, not to get involved with this man. Ignoring the warning bells clanging inside her head, she wanted to be that woman so very badly, if only for just one night. Sabrina hadn't known she'd signed a pact with the devil himself because she could never have imagined that sex could be so wonderful, so gentle and loving. Lucas had made her feel like she was someone who deserved to be treated with care and respect. Sabrina had felt it in his touch, in his kisses and finally, as he moved inside her, the emotions carrying her away on a tide of pleasure so intense, she thought her heart would burst. And then, as if someone had flipped a switch, she was back in her reality. The reality of a serial killer, a woman who had taken the life of six men and who was planning to take another. Sneaking out of his house and his life had seemed appropriate, she hadn't been able to wait for him to wake up. How could she explain that they could never have more than this one night? Any explanation would have been a lie and, given the emotions they had felt, she just couldn't bring herself to add to the growing list of lies she'd told him. Sabrina knew that Lucas had been as affected by their love making as she'd been. Every time he'd touched her, she'd known, had felt it in every kiss. But he deserved so much more. She was horribly aware that there was nothing she could give him, at least nothing more than sharing her body with him. Still, she felt compelled to let him know just how much their time together had meant to her, so she wrote the note. Tiptoeing quietly back to the bedroom, Sabrina had taken a last look at the sleeping man in the bed and then had slipped out of the house quietly.

After Sabrina had gotten home, she had toyed with the idea of finishing her last assignment and then go back to Baltimore and Lucas. She'd spent hours playing out that scenario in her mind, seeing herself being with him, maybe get married and having a couple of children, finally having a chance at living the life of a normal person. But she soon realised, she was kidding herself by pretending she could commit another murder and then go and live happily ever after. A bitter laugh at the realisation that she was really completely off her head had put an end to such nonsense. She was who she was, a product of circumstance perhaps, at least in the beginning. Maybe, in the beginning, Sabrina could have gotten over the attack, could have gotten on with her life and perhaps then, she could have had that normal life. If she hadn't been alone, if she had access to help from experts to try and deal with the attack. If, if, if! What use was it to think like that? She had been alone and no one had helped. Who would have believed her? The authorities? The Police? The Senator was a powerful man with connections, she'd seen it when her mother's death had been presented as a tragic accident. In the end, it hadn't mattered because that chance had vanished the day she had come across a news article about a serial child abuser who had been convicted of countless rapes and indecency against children. He'd gotten a life sentence for his crimes. Reading that article had awakened something inside her, something dark; a fury at the injustice of it all as she thought about the pain and suffering these children had endured. Her already feeble grip on her will to try and overcome what had been done to her finally snapped and her life had changed irrevocably.

With an almost manic fervour, Sabrina had spent weeks surfing the dark web, digging up information about secret clubs, paedophile rings and specialist websites catering for every abhorrent and sick fantasy. By being exposed such horror over many weeks, her thoughts had become more and more twisted, setting the stage for a plan to begin to take shape about ridding the world of some of these sick bastards. Sabrina had come across the first of her targets by chance. Finding a particularly horrendous site, she'd managed to infiltrate the chat room by pretending to be one of them. This one guy revelled in describing everything he did to those kids in great detail. At one point, it got so bad that Sabrina had to log out, throwing up in her bathroom until there was nothing left inside of her. Although they were careful not to mention any real names, locations or any other kind of personal information, when she logged on couple of days later, she put her hacking skills to good use and traced him. Once she had his IP address, finding out where he lived had been easy. These bastards thought that by hiding on the dark web, no one was ever going to discover their real identity.

Preparing for the first assignment had taken months. She'd spent weeks researching crime scene data, read hundreds of articles on forensic science, from basic finger printing, to blood splatter science and the latest development of sophisticated DNA tests. Reading up on the human anatomy, she learned about weak spots, where a slow bleed-out would result in maximum pain without causing immediate death. Sabrina spent many days figuring out how to avoid any kind of trace, be it DNA or other evidence that could lead the cops back to her. She was already living under an assumed identity since using her real name evoked too many horrors. After she'd escaped, she'd hidden away in cheap motels, where no one asked questions. It wasn't until much later that she thought to get a new ID. She'd thought that she could start over, pretend the past never happened and redo her life. No one knew her so that was one problem less. She didn't know if the Senator had reported her as missing all those years ago. If he had, the police would have most certainly collected samples for DNA identification, in case she ever turned up as a dead Jane Doe somewhere. Still, she wasn't prepared to take any chances and, in the end, she came up with the idea of the bodysuit. Watching one of many videos of CSI investigations, she had noticed that the Techs always wore protective clothing so as not to contaminate a crime scene. Since she couldn't very well turn up clad in a white boiler suit, she'd racked her brain for a solution. It came to her quite by chance when she clicked on a news article about some Hollywood starlet who'd gotten herself into hot water by blabbing about having an affair with a famous actor who, at the time, had been married. Sabrina wasn't interested in the fall out of this tawdry tale but what caught her attention, was the tight-fitting body suit the girl wore as she enjoyed her five minutes in the limelight. Designing a suit that fulfilled her requirements had been the next step and once she was happy with it, she found a website based in Hong Kong where such items could be ordered without any questions being asked. Giving instructions on the specific type of materials she wanted, she'd placed the order and two weeks later, the suit had arrived. Sabrina could recall every detail of the time she put it on for the very first time. It fitted like a glove and had been made to her exact instructions. The garment had been constructed from one piece of material which had three layers of different fabrics. The inner and outer layer was made from a breathable but moisture absorbing fabric, much like the stuff garments for athletes were made of. It was the middle layer that was special. It would shield her from any spills by acting as a complete barrier, preventing any of her own DNA from escaping. The fabric had been developed in the early nineties, its intended purpose primarily for medical use to protect surgeons and other medical staff from being infected by patients' blood and other body fluids. At the time, this had been a revolutionary product, Aids contamination being the biggest factor in its development. Sabrina had read articles about the fabric and had been impressed by its protective properties, the promotional video showing clearly that even when pressure was applied onto the outer side of the fabric, nothing would penetrate and thus provide perfect protection. She knew enough about forensics to know that even the smallest of traces, such as skin cells or droplets of sweat were sufficient to extract DNA. The one and only seam that held the suit together had been double stitched so that nothing could pass through the needle holes. During all of this time, as she made her preparations, she'd kept track of the target, getting to know his daily life in detail. Finding out that he lived alone made the formulation of a plan that much easier. She'd gone as far as actually staking out his address in order to try and figure out the best way to get access. But the first time she'd laid eyes on him, Sabrina realised that she would need to find a way to subdue him. He was a big man and no way could she overpower him without some sort of help. She didn't like guns, never even fired one so that option was out. Once again, she searched the net and after two exhausting days of hunting around for a solution, she at last found what she was looking for. When she stumbled across a video demonstrating Tasers, a tool used by law enforcement agencies around the world, Sabrina was astonished at the simplicity of the device. With a Taser, she could avoid close contact since it could be fired from up to fifteen feet away. The handy little device worked on the basis of shooting two metal darts into the target, delivering an electric shock strong enough to subdue even the biggest of men. It was also small enough to fit in her bag. The final purchase were some plastic zip-ties, the kind she'd seen police use to handcuff felons. Now her kit was complete. She was ready.

Chapter 17

John Donaldson was in the middle of preparing his dinner when he heard a knock on the door. Peeking out through the curtains, he saw a young woman standing there, a clipboard clutched in one hand.

"Damn!" He muttered, debating whether or not to open the door. Taking a second glance, he saw that she was a slim, good looking woman, though he couldn't quite make out her features in the low evening light. Shrugging to himself, he figured it would brighten up his evening, having a chat with someone so appealing and went and opened his door.

"Mr. Donaldson?" She had a very nice melodic voice which he liked, so he nodded.

"I'm sorry to disturb you, Sir. My name is Jane Foster, I'm from your insurance company. We've received your claim regarding some damage done by an attempted burglary and wondered whether I could have a quick look around?"

Jane smiled at him and John figured it would do no harm to let her have a quick look since he'd been waiting to hear from them for over a week.

"Sure, come on in." He said and stepped aside to let her in, closing the door behind her.

As she passed by him, he picked up the faint scent of her perfume. It smelled really nice and now that he'd seen her close up, he could see she was younger than he'd first thought, more a girl than a woman. His dick stirred in his pants as he thought of the fun he could have with her. He'd just bet she'd be great in the sack. She stood a few feet away from him, an innocent smile on her face as she fumbled in her large bag, presumably looking for a pen. He couldn't quite see what she pulled out but seconds later, he felt a tremendous pain shooting through his chest. He cried out, too shocked to figure out what had just happened. Then another bolt of pain shot through him and he felt himself fall before passing out.

When he came to, he was confused to find himself in his bath tub, completely naked and soaking wet. He tried to move but when he couldn't, he realised his hands were tied behind his back. Looking down at his ankles, he saw that they too were tied up, his knees bent at an awkward angle, effectively wedging him in the tub. That's when he started to panic. He tried to open his mouth, momentarily confused when he couldn't. Just at the edge of his field of vision, he could see the ends of the tape that covered his mouth. Renewed panic shot through him and as he finally raised his eyes, he saw Jane standing in front of the tub, a cold smile on her face. When he'd let her in the house, she'd been wearing a pant suit, now though she had on what looked like an overall, except this one was skin tight, covering her from head to toe. A flash caught his eye and that's when he saw the blade in her hand. Fear pulsed through him, making it hard to breathe.

"I see you're awake." Jane said, her previously gentle voice cold and hard.

Eyes bulging, John tried to move but only managed to slip a little further into the tub. The woman laughed at his pathetic efforts to try and get as far away from her as he could.

"You can struggle all you like, you won't get anywhere."

Taking a step closer to the tub, she studied him for a brief moment.

"How do you like it, John? Having all your movements restrained, being at someone's mercy?"

Absorbing her words, he finally understood what was happening. Somehow this bitch had found out about his activities and was hell bent on payback. With sudden clarity he realised that he would die in his tub and that thought made him squeal, though all that could be heard was a muffled sound. He started crying, tears and snot running down his face but he didn't care. He didn't want to die, not like this but he also knew that the woman in front of him would show no mercy. Before he saw it, she was on him, the fluid motion of her arm as she brought the blade down almost beautiful. The blade penetrated his right side, just under his ribs and she gave a little twist before pulling it out again. In shock, he watched as blood came seeping out of the wound before the pain hit. He almost passed out, not noticing when she came back and sliced deeply across his belly, exposing his innards. He looked down at his glistening entrails, the pain so intense he couldn't even scream. The third time the blade touched him, she slashed a large X across his chest, not particularly deep, just enough to let more blood flow.

"Your final kiss." She hissed.

Then she stood back, watching him with a cold stare before turning to the sink and rinsing the blade under hot water, the flow red from his blood. Despite the pain, he looked on as she pulled out a wipe, cleaning the steel with care before flipping it shut and putting it away.

"Well, I'll be off then, John. Hope you rot in hell, you sick fuck!"

Too far gone to do more than moan, he watched as she left the bathroom without a backward glance and then closed his eyes, waiting for death to release him.

***

After getting home that night, she'd undressed and turned on the shower. As she looked at her reflection in the bathroom mirror which had started to steam up with the heat from the shower, she didn't recognise the face staring back at her. Her stomach heaved as realisation at what she'd done dawned on her. She was a killer! Dropping to her knees, she emptied the contents of her stomach until she had nothing left in her. Feeling completely numb, she sat on the cold bathroom floor as she tried to deal with the emotional fall-out. By the time she got in the shower, the hot water had run out but she forced herself to stay under the icy spray, hoping to feel something, anything, again. With her teeth chattering, she finally switched off the water and towelled her shivering body. For two days after, Sabrina had stayed locked away in her apartment. She'd spent the first day in bed, wanting to block it all out. She'd taken a couple of pills to help her sleep and every time she woke, she took another to sink back into blessed unconsciousness. On the second day, she finally got up. Preparing something to eat, having a shower and getting dressed helped dispel the last of the foggy haze in her head. Getting back into some sort of normalcy helped but what she really was doing, was refusing to think about the horror of what she'd done. Her refusal to watch the news or even go online was all part of the process of denial. If she didn't think about it, she could stash away the memory of that night, much in the same way she'd dealt with memories of the night she'd been violated. From this day on, she would never be a 'normal' person again. She had crossed a line, from which there was no come back. She'd stepped onto a path that would carry her in a certain direction, no deviations allowed. Over the years, she'd dealt with each assignment in a similar way although she had less trouble getting over her actions with every killing, her mind growing used to the fact that she took lives. She always had a couple of days after each of them where she felt out of sync but the horror of the first one never returned. Sabrina never again analysed her feelings, avoiding any kind of guilt by justifying her actions with the warped notion that she was actually doing the right thing by getting rid of this scum of the earth. Until she met Lucas. Now, as she acknowledged what she'd been doing all these years, what it had made of her, she knew that it was far too late to change anything. Knowing that didn't make any difference though. She had chosen that particular way forward so many years ago, there would be no giving up now, no way to rectify any of the things she'd done. As realisation dawned on her, she also knew that soon, all of it would be over. Sabrina mourned the sixteen-year old girl she'd once been but refused to dwell on what could have been. She had one final assignment, one she'd been reluctant to carry out for so long but the time had finally come to see this thing through to the bitter end.

Chapter 18

Lucas sat at his desk, cradling a cup of coffee, or rather the black sludge that passed for coffee in the office, feeling a little sorry for himself. His head was still pounding, his churning stomach adding to his misery. For days, he'd buried himself in work, hoping that by keeping busy, his mind would stop going over and over as to why Sabrina had disappeared out of his life. Again. According to her note, she had enjoyed herself. No, scratch that, she'd had the best night of her life and yet, she'd run from him. Try as he might, he couldn't understand what had driven her away without leaving any contact details, not even a goodbye. Last night, fed up with the whole screwed up situation, he'd decided to drown his sorry ass. So, he'd gotten drunk off his face, had tried and failed miserably to hook up with some blonde in one of the bars because he just couldn't bring himself to take another woman to his bed.

Loud voices and the crashing of the office door being opened with some force pulled him from his miserable thoughts as he watched Dan march in, a young guy following behind, face red with exertion as he carried two large boxes in his arms, trying to see where he was going without dropping them.

"Put them over there, get your sorry self a chair and start working!" Dan instructed the poor sap, a nasty tone in his voice.

Lucas looked on in amazement at the unfolding scene.

"What the hell is going on here?"

He had never seen Dan so worked up.

His partner turned to him, a look of disgust on his face.

"This sorry excuse for an agent here" he pointed a finger at the young man sitting at the empty desk, "has withheld possibly vital evidence."

"How so?" Lucas asked, puzzled.

"He was part of the search unit going into Peter Saunders' office to get the paperwork." Dan sighed. "Only, instead of bringing it in, he went off on vacation for three weeks!"

Lucas took another sip of his horrible coffee which, despite its taste and appearance, was making its way through his system, finally starting to make him feel a little more human. Before he could say anything, Dan continued.

"Three weeks! Pissed off to Hawaii and forgot all about it!"

"It was my honeymoon ..." The young guy was trying to interject but Dan was having none of it.

"I don't care! You know as well as I do, evidence comes first, no matter what. What were you thinking?"

The other guy, whose name Lucas still didn't know but who very obviously was a newbie, opened his mouth but Dan waved a hand at him in resignation.

"No, don't answer that! We all know where your mind was! But I tell you this, Samuel L. Jackson, you're lucky to keep your damn job!"

He turned and sat down at his own desk, finally looking at Lucas who sat there, his mouth hanging open in surprise.

"Samuel L. Jackson? You are fucking kidding me!"

Despite his anger, Dan joined in the laughter that Lucas could no longer keep in.

"I know, right?" Grinning, Dan turned to the man in question.

"Explain to Special Agent Lucas Green why your Mamma gave you that particular name."

Lucas bent slightly forward, eager to hear how a ginger haired, lanky guy ended up being named after the famous black actor. Samuel's pale cheeks turned bright red.

"Well, see my Mom is Samuel L. Jackson's number one fan. She's seen every one of his movies countless times, she's even met the man and when she met my Dad, she knew it was destiny, because of his last name. So of course, when they had me, there was only one name she would choose." He shrugged his skinny shoulders. "I guess it could have been worse."

"You reckon?" Lucas asked, laughing at the explanation.

"Yeah! Just imagine, if she'd been a fan of the Jackson five, I could have ended up with several names because I'm convinced my Mom is crazy enough to have named me after all five brothers!"

Lucas shook his head, still laughing. "I suppose so. At least she picked a good actor!"

"Get to work!" Dan barked, trying to sound threatening but not quite able to keep a grin off his face.

***

A couple of hours later, Lucas looked up from the report on a drug bust they had been working on to find Samuel standing in front of him, holding some paperwork.

"What is it?"

"Well, Sir, I found this."

He handed Lucas the papers without further explanation. Lucas took them and when he realised what he was looking at, he drew in a sharp breath.

"Well I'll be damned! Hey Dan, look what Mr. Hollywood found!"

Dan ambled over and took the papers from Lucas. Scanning the two pages, he let out a whistle when he came to the end.

"Evie Templeton? What the fuck?"

The papers in question were a copy of a contract between Peter Saunders and a Miss Evie Templeton, an accredited accountant, detailing what services she would offer to sort out various problems with Saunders' accounts.

The implication hit both men at the same time. Was it possible that the X murderer was a woman? There was no doubt in Lucas's mind that they were looking at the first real clue in this messed up investigation. Stunned, he stared at Dan, a similar expression on his partner's face. Looking at the signature at the bottom of the second page, Lucas felt a shiver running down his spine. Something about that signature bothered him but he couldn't quite figure out what. He knew the name was fake, they'd established that much. So, what was it? Shaking his head, he put the papers down and looked up at the two men standing in front of him.

"Okay then, here's what's going to happen. We re-interview all of the staff who work at the main store. And I mean every last one of them!" He sent a stern look in Samuel's direction. "We need to know if Saunders ever met with this Evie Templeton at his office. With a bit of luck, we'll get a description." Feeling encouraged at having something to get their teeth into, he and Dan looked at each other, both grinning.

"Let's do it!"

He turned to Samuel.

"You carry on looking through the rest of the boxes, see if you can find anything else. Good work, man."

Smiling at the small praise, Samuel turned and pulled another file out of the box beside of him.

Lucas and Dan arrived a short while later at the main site of the small chain of Drycleaners, where Saunders had kept his office. Saunders had been too tight-fisted to have a secretary but if Lucas knew anything about low paid, overworked staff, he knew they would know plenty about what had been going on in the small office. Sure enough, one of the women recalled exactly such a meeting, when asked about it by Lucas. He'd been hard pushed not to either laugh or curse when she'd told him her name. Nora Roberts? What was going on with all the famous namesakes today? Focusing back on the interview, he didn't dare look at Dan because he just knew his partner would also have a hard time keeping a straight face.

"I do recall it, yes indeed." Nora said, nodding her head earnestly.

"The woman was young and very beautiful. Mr. Saunders was practically salivating as he led her through to the back." She paused, obviously recalling the scene in her mind.

"Could you give us a more detailed description of the woman?" Lucas kept his voice calm despite his growing excitement that finally, they would have an idea of what their killer looked like.

"I'm not sure exactly what she looked like, because Mr. Saunders didn't introduce her. Like I said, she was a pretty young thing, long red hair, although she'd put it up in some kind of bun at the back of her neck, you know? All business like, what with her suit and briefcase."

Dan was scribbling furiously in his notebook, trying to keep up with the fast-talking woman.

"Could you estimate how tall she was? Was she slim, any particular features you recall about her?" Lucas asked with a smile.

"Well now, let me think."

The woman scratched her hair as she tried to remember.

"I'd guess she was about five eight, slim but not skinny. I don't recall anything about her other than that she was really pretty."

"Okay, that's great. Did she visit more than once?"

Nora shook her head. "No, that was the only time I saw her here but I do know that Mr. Saunders did meet with her again."

Lucas's eyebrows shot up. "How do you know that?"

"Because he told me. Boasted that he was going to have dinner with her, at his house. Apparently, she wanted to go over some figures with him."

Nora raised an eyebrow, indicating that she thought Saunders had ben hoping for some extra services from Miss Templeton. Bet he hadn't thought for a moment just what extras she dished out that night, Lucas thought grimly.

Looking over at Dan, he gave a small nod before turning to back to Nora.

"Thank you so much, Nora. You've been very helpful."

"You're welcome, honey. I'm sorry I can't tell you more." Nora shrugged apologetically.

"No, like I said, any information is welcome. You have a good day now." Lucas shook her hand.

Once back in the car, he looked over at Dan, a grim expression on his face.

"I did not see that coming!"

He shook his head, still trying to process the fact that in all likelihood, they now had the first solid lead, a description and the fact the killer was female! A young and, by all accounts, a very pretty one at that! Lucas had trouble getting his mind to accept what they'd just heard. Judging by the look on Dan's face, he wasn't alone. He could see his partner trying to process the information.

"So, what we're thinking is that when Saunders met with her at his house, she went there specifically to kill him."

It was a statement rather than a question and Lucas nodded. Dan mulled that over for a moment.

"And yet, none of the neighbours saw her arrive or leave. Damn, how are we going to go from here?"

That was a very good question. They'd already checked for CCTV in the neighbourhood but since it was a quiet, unassuming area, there hadn't been any. If Saunders had lived in a more urban setting, they might have gotten lucky and would have had some footage.

Lucas picked up his phone.

"Samuel, get that contract down to forensics, see if they can lift a print or some other DNA."

By the time they were back at the office, Sam was waiting for them.

"Any luck?" Dan asked with a hopeful look on his face.

"Yes and no. We have a print that doesn't belong to the victim. Forensics ran it through all available data bases and came up with nothing. Whoever she is, she's not got any previous."

"Fuck!"

Dan huffed and Lucas couldn't have agreed more. Anger rose unexpectedly. Every time they thought they had something, it turned out to be of no use. But that wasn't entirely true. Working on the assumption the killer was male had been wrong. Lucas still found it hard to imagine what sort of person, let alone a woman, could commit so many horrendous murders. He wasn't being sexist in any way but the statistics proved that female serial killers were rare, although not unheard of. This woman was extremely clever, she knew as much about forensics as any of them and up until now, had left not a single trace. Despite the fact that she was a cold-blooded killer, he had to admit to having some respect for her. Her ability to prepare and plan for all circumstances, covering all aspects of a murder and her subsequent disappearance not only made her super smart but also extremely dangerous. Being this thorough meant she had no intention of ever getting caught and who knew how many more victims would meet their grisly end at her hands? Casting his mind back over the five other files he'd studied in detail, there was no pattern to the geographical location where her victims had been found. In three of the six cases, she'd killed them in their own bath tub, presumably to avoid getting contaminated by the victims' blood. Again, a very smart move. The only other connection between them all was the fact that they were child abusers. Wham! It hit him like a sledgehammer! Of course, now that he thought about it in the correct order, he realised how she chose her victims. He knew enough about how paedophile rings operated, often under ground or on the dark web, fiercely secretive and covering their tracks. Lucas knew from what Joe had said that she was computer savvy, but what if she was more than that? Hackers were known to be able to infiltrate just about any site, on the internet or on the dark web. Hell, even Government systems had been hacked more than once, resulting in high profile court cases.

"Dan!"

He waved his partner over before picking up the phone and putting it on loud speaker. Dan ambled over.

"What's up?"

Lucas held up a finger as Joe answered.

"Joe, I need a favour."

"Shoot."

"Get all previous X Murder files and check to see if all of them had access to the internet. If they did, have the computers sent over here and see if they too had been tampered with."

"Okay. Anything else I should be looking for?"

Lucas liked the fact that Joe seemed to understand his way of thinking. He himself wasn't knowledgeable enough to figure out how to access the dark web but he thought Joe could.

"Yeah, can you check for any activity in other areas?"

Dan's eyebrows shot up in astonishment. Joe was silent for a moment.

"Am I right in thinking that there may be a link? Like a common website?"

Lucas sighed. "Well, some websites were already checked and so far, we haven't been able to find anything but I was hoping you could." He waited, hoping his instincts about Joe were correct.

"I'm coming up."

Joe hung up without another word and Lucas put the phone down with a satisfied grin on his face. Oh yeah! Joe knew what he was asking.

"What are you doing?" Dan asked, confusion on his face.

"I'll explain when Joe gets here. But if I'm right and Joe does what I hope he will do, we may just find a concrete connection for all six victims."

Five minutes later, Joe marched into the office and pulled up a chair in front of Lucas's desk.

Dan and Sam came over to join them as Lucas explained his thought process and what he wanted Joe to do. Joe sat for a moment, his eyes on Lucas who returned his gaze, an unspoken question hanging between them.

"You do realise that what you are asking me to do is illegal, right?" Joe sounded very matter of fact, much to Lucas's satisfaction.

"I do. If you're okay with that, I would prefer if you did whatever you have to do to get the information we need in private."

"So, let's say I find something, something to prove the connection, you realise we wouldn't be able to use any of it as evidence, right? You know, illegal isn't usually allowed." He finished with a grin.

"If you find anything, I'll go and see the Boss and if it means finding the killer, we'll find a way to use the information." Lucas sighed. "We need to stop her."

Joe gasped. "Her? The killer is a woman?"

Lucas had forgotten that Joe wasn't up to speed with the latest developments and filled him in.

"Well, fuck!"

Momentarily lost for words, Joe rubbed a hand across his chin. Shaking his head, he got up.

"I'll do what I can, Lucas. But shit, a woman?" Mumbling to himself, he turned and left the office.

Lucas knew exactly how he felt.

Chapter 19

Having had a few days off thanks to the excuse of having to attend her imaginary Grandmother's funeral, Sabrina was back at work. Outwardly, she played the role of the grieving granddaughter whilst trying to figure out how, where and when she could get the Senator alone. She knew she needed to get a plan of action into place sooner rather than later. She felt an urgency to set up and finish this assignment, an urgency she'd never had before. Somehow, she knew, that time was running out for her. A feeling of desolation swept through her, a knowledge that judgement day wasn't too far in the distance. Making peace with that thought, accepting that one way or another, she would soon arrive at the end of the line, wasn't something she'd prepared for. She'd never thought about the repercussions of her actions or how it would all come to an end but now, she felt a darkness descending. She knew with absolute clarity that soon, she would face her own end. A thought that frightened her and yet at the same time, allowed her some peace. At least she would be free, no longer chained to memories so horrendous and dark, they had coloured all of her adult life and made her what she was. So, she made preparations, spending long hours into the night, tapping away at her computer. Once she'd finished, she felt calm, a new resolve steeling her mind, helping her to focus on the task in hand.

It was a few days later, as Sabrina sat typing away at her desk in the Senator's office, that the idea suddenly presented itself. She'd been mindlessly working away, transferring details of donations onto the system. The wedding had generated a lot of interest nationwide and donations were pouring in, keeping her and the rest of the office busy. Looking at the screen before her, a clear and almost fully formed plan unfolded in her mind, excitement coursing through her at the relative simplicity of it. Sabrina had thought of dozens of ways to get the Senator alone, but it seemed he was always surrounded by aides, office staff or other politicians. Up until now, she'd not found a way to make sure that not only would she be alone with him but also have enough time to do what she needed to without being disturbed. Itching to get started, she kept an eye on the clock, wishing for her workday to finish so she could go home and set the wheels in motion. The day seemed to stretch into eternity but at last, she was free to go home and prepare. Once home, she made a large pot of coffee and set to work. By four in the morning, she'd set up the preliminaries, it would take another couple of days and then she would be ready. Still waiting for the one item she'd ordered a couple of days ago, Sabrina knew she couldn't proceed until it was safely in her hands.

Two days later, Sabrina arrived at her desk, on time as usual. Despite the lack of sleep, she'd worked until the early hours over the past couple of nights, she was keyed up. Today she would see if the first step of her plan was going to work! Making idle conversation with Sonia, she waited for her to open her emails. Sonia always did that task first, sorting through the Senator's inbox, passing some of the emails on to the relevant people, handling some herself. Sabrina watched her covertly and knew the exact moment, Sonia read one particular email.

"Oh my, this is interesting!" Her chubby cheeks glowed with excitement.

Sabrina feigned interest as she got up and walked over to Sonia's desk.

"What is it?"

Sonia glanced up at her, thought for a moment, then shrugged her shoulders.

"I guess I can show you, Katie. You've proved yourself to be a good worker and, if this email is genuine, relates directly to your job."

She paused for effect and Sabrina made sure her face showed the appropriate amount of interest. Bending down, she read the email and straightened.

"Goodness! I see what you mean, Sonia."

Refraining from saying anymore, she watched the other woman's face. Mentally keeping her fingers crossed, she waited for Sonia to follow her usual mode of work and wasn't disappointed.

"I'll check this out and then speak to the Senator about it." Sounding excited, Sonia turned to Sabrina, who by now was back at her desk.

"We'll keep this to ourselves for now."

It wasn't a question, Sabrina knew, so she nodded and gave Sonia the thumbs up.

"Sure thing! My lips are sealed!"

She grinned at the other woman and went back to work. Now she had to wait. Tonight, she would add another building block to her plan, setting the scene for her final assignment.

On her way home, she made a detour to the post office to check her mail box and stood before the wall lined with metal boxes, key in hand, her breath coming out in sharp bursts. With shaking fingers, she inserted the key and opened the box, staring at the innocent looking brown envelope waiting for her. With a fortifying breath, she pulled out the padded envelope, knowing what its contents signified. Still shaking, she stowed the package away in her bag and slowly made her way outside, standing still for a moment, not hearing the noise of the traffic around her and completely oblivious to the people rushing past her. Navigating the evening rush hour traffic took all of her concentration but once home, she dropped her bag and went straight to the fridge, pulled out the Tequila and took several large gulps, hoping the alcohol would calm her screaming nerves. Ten minutes later, she still felt shaky, but Sabrina couldn't afford to get drunk, not tonight. Her mind was already in turmoil, too much alcohol would only make things worse. With a determined huff, she got up and put the bottle back.

Grabbing her bag, she pulled out the envelope and opened it, emptying its content into her hand. The small item in her palm looked harmless enough but Sabrina couldn't control the shudder that ran through her at the thought of its meaning. With a resigned sigh, she put it back in its packaging and stuffed it into her bag. She had a lot of work to do, now was not the time to think about things she couldn't and wouldn't change. Finalising the smaller details of her plan had to be her main focus and so she went to work, putting the envelope and its content firmly out of her mind.

***

Sonia Whitmore was excited. She'd just finished a meeting with the Senator, discussing the potential new donor. She'd printed out the latest email from Mr. Prescott, as was her habit since Senator Heffner didn't have time to scroll through hundreds of emails.

"I take it you've checked this Mr. Prescott out?" The Senator asked, taking off his reading glasses and fixing his gaze on her.

"Indeed, I have, Sir. Mr. Larry Prescott is what he says he is, a legal arms dealer for the past twenty years and a member of the NRA."

The Senator's eyes lit up at that. "Excellent!"

Sonia knew that he'd been trying to find a way to get associated with the big names in the NRA but had yet to achieve that particular ambition. A staunch supporter of current gun laws, the Senator knew that if he ever wanted to make an attempt at running for the top job, he would need some serious backers. Campaigns were expensive, he knew that from previous experience. The funds it took to run for President were something else altogether. What money had been spent to get him this far was peanuts in comparison.

"He was in the Army for five years. Since then, he's been very successful and as far as I can tell, has the sort of funds you are looking for, Sir. Not to mention his contacts."

Sonia looked at the man opposite her.

"His request for the first meeting to be in private seems reasonable to me. From what I've found, he's not someone who seeks publicity. I didn't find anything on him with regard to a social life, he's divorced and currently unattached. He seems to be a very private man which is good because there are no scandals or any other harmful news attached to his name."

Sonia added the last with confidence. It never occurred to her that this would be odd in any way. After all, many rich people tended to shun the limelight.

The Senator nodded. "Okay, so he wants to meet at the Four Seasons?"

"That's correct. He's overseas at the moment but says he'll be in DC by Friday."

Repeating the words from Mr. Prescott's email, she continued.

"Apparently, he usually takes the Royal Suite, since it is on the top floor and only accessible with a special elevator key. It would appear that security is as important to him as it is to you, Sir."

The Senator sat quietly for a moment, then nodded.

"What's in my diary for Friday? Any other engagements?"

Sonia shook her head. "There was a dinner planned with your wife, Sir but I'm sure, Mrs. Hefner will understand the importance of this meeting."

The Senator waved a hand dismissingly.

"Of course, she does. Confirm the meeting with Mr. Prescott. This is a great opportunity and one I can't afford to miss. Just make sure this is kept quiet, we don't want anything to get out before we have concrete plans. Once an agreement between Mr. Prescott and myself has been made, we'll see about who needs to know."

His tone indicated that their meeting was over and Sonia rose from her seat.

"Of course, Sir! I'll see to it personally." Leaving the Senator to get on with his work, she gathered her papers and left.

Chapter 20

It had taken a few days, but finally Joe came into the office, a file in his hand. Lucas motioned both Dan and Sam over to his desk, wanting them to hear what Joe had uncovered.

"What have you got for us?"

Lucas couldn't quite hide his impatience, he needed a break and he needed it fast.

Joe sat down and opened his file.

"So, it turns out all six of the victims had computers but ours was the only one who'd been accessed by, what we assume, is the killer. I spoke to all the other FBI offices who have files on the X murderer and their IT people checked them out thoroughly. The only common thing was that all of the computers had been used for various paedophile networks. Not news, I know. Unfortunately, we couldn't establish a connection between all six of the victims but four of them used the same website on a regular basis, visiting chatrooms etc."

Joe paused for a minute, rubbing a hand over his face.

"Man, I gotta tell you, these were some sick bastards. I only looked briefly but I know I'll have nightmares for a very long time."

His last words came out bleakly and Lucas felt a pang of sympathy for the young man sitting in front of him.

"I'm sorry to hear that but I really appreciate your efforts, Joe. I know this shit is hard to deal with."

"Thanks." Joe nodded. "I have passed the details onto the people dealing with that sort of thing." He shook his head. "I don't know how they can do this kind of work, I really can't!"

Lucas understood the sentiment. "Well, let's just be glad that they do. From what I know, they take down such websites on a daily basis but it seems those sickos just set up new ones and carry on as before."

All four men sat in silence for a while, trying to absorb the awful awareness of what was happening out there in the world and wondering how they could possibly make a difference. Lucas shook his head, pulling himself out of these horrible thoughts.

"I know this is hard on all of us but we need to keep our focus on the killer. Just because she kills sick bastards, doesn't mean she's exempt from the law."

"If she didn't access the other computers, what was she doing on the one from our victim?" Sam asked and Lucas was impressed with his thought process.

"It seems most likely that she erased all traces of their business transactions." He said. "Presumably they would have emailed to keep in touch?"

He looked at Joe in question.

"I agree, that would seem plausible." Joe nodded in agreement.

Lucas thought about that for a moment.

"I guess we can assume that the other victims were approached in a different manner. Otherwise she would have had to go through their computers too."

He paused as he tried to understand how this female killer managed to get close enough to her victims. It seemed that she used various methods and he had to admit that hooking someone with the lure of getting money back of the IRS was a stroke of genius, particularly someone like Peter Saunders. He had been a well known cheapskate, saving money wherever he could, most notably on the welfare of his staff. Several of the staff they'd interviewed had told them that health insurance was only paid after a years' employment. Lucas was once again astonished at the depth of research the woman had to have carried out to know just how to get to the man.

He turned to Sam. "Has Nora been to see the sketch artist?"

Sam nodded. "She came in this morning, hopefully we should have something later today."

Lucas wasn't convinced that they would get a full, detailed face. From what he recalled, Nora had seen the woman only very briefly and hadn't remembered any specific details. But he had to hope that the facial reconstruction guys knew their job and would provide him with something he could use. But until the picture arrived, there wasn't much else they could do so they ended their impromptu meeting and Joe left to go back to his office. Dan and Sam both retuned to their own desk to get on with their work.

It was several hours later, when his computer pinged, indicating the arrival of the sketch. Lucas waited impatiently for the picture to download, scanning through the brief report the artist had included. Just as he had feared, the details given by the witness had been sketchy to say the least but the artist had done what he could. Finally, the download was complete and Lucas found himself staring at the picture of a woman, who was young and certainly beautiful but not much else by way of distinguishing features. The artist had mentioned that he'd reconstructed the face from the description given to him by the witness, who had really only seen her in profile. He also said that the colour of the eyes had been guess work since Nora couldn't recall what colour they were. The witness had been very clear on the fact that she remembered the woman having high cheekbones and a high forehead. Apologising for his guess work, the artist signed off, wishing them good luck. Lucas chuckled grimly. He would need all the luck in the world, that much was certain. Scrutinising the details of the face staring back at him, he felt a tingle running down his spine. There was a hint of familiarity about this woman's face in the set of her eyes and the high cheek bones. He shook his head, trying to keep an open mind and not reading anything into this that was non-existent. And yet, he couldn't shake the feeling. Out of nowhere, Sabrina's face popped up in his minds' eye. She had pronounced cheek bones and a high forehead but that was where the similarity ended. For a start, the killer had red hair whereas Sabrina was dark and he wasn't likely to forget the intensity of her beautiful green eyes. Of course, he knew perfectly well that appearances could be changed easily enough. Lucas sat back in his chair, shaking his head at his thoughts. Sure, Sabrina was a young woman, but her very apparent shyness and clearly noticeable naivety didn't exactly scream serial killer! He grimaced at the crazy direction his thoughts had taken! He'd been thinking about her far too often and now, his tired brain was seeing things that bore no correlation to the facts. Stressed and overworked, he didn't remember the nightmare he'd had, just before he'd woken up to find Sabrina gone. He also didn't think to make a connection between the fact that she'd given away very little about herself during either of their meetings or her sudden disappearance on that first night, shortly after he'd told her what he did for a living. The face staring back at him from his screen belonged to a person with a very sick mind, beautiful or not. With a sigh, Lucas closed the picture, sick of getting nowhere fast with this fucked up investigation. The face could belong to any number of thousands of women out there, but it most certainly did not belong to Sabrina. He really needed a vacation or, better still, see a fucking shrink to sort his head out!

Focusing his mind back on the job, he sent the picture to the other FBI offices with files on the X murders with a detailed explanation as to what they had uncovered so far. Perhaps one of the other offices had further details to add to the investigation. Since they had all assumed, wrongly as it turned out, that the killer was male, he thought that with this new piece of information, others would again look at their own files. It was a long shot but if experience had taught him anything, it was this. Sooner or later, most killers slipped up and left evidence, even if it was seemingly unimportant. If other similar information came to light, there was a much better chance that they would catch up with the woman and put a stop to the killings.

Chapter 21

After yet another disappointing week, Lucas decided to put all thoughts of work out of his mind for the coming weekend. Maybe he would go hiking, something he hadn't done for a very long time. An image of him and his father appeared in his mind. They'd gone hiking a lot when he was young. His Dad had taught him how to fish, as well as how to distinguish edible berries from those who could make you either sick or worse and other fauna that could be found, should you know where to look. During the warmer months, they' taken a tent but in winter, they would hire a cabin for the weekend. Lucas smiled at the memory of those times spent with his father along with a tinge of sadness at the loss of his Dad. They'd been close and his death had hit him hard. He still had all the gear for a weekend in the country stored in his garage and the thought of getting away for just a couple of days put a smile in his face. Yes, he would check it all out once home and then he'd get in his car and drive somewhere where there were no people, only nature and wilderness, giving him a chance to recharge. The reports from the other FBI agencies had come back after he'd sent the picture of the killer. Not one of them had anything to add, none of them had found any links to a mysterious female killer, no matter how hard they rechecked every detail. It was enough to drive a Saint to madness and Lucas had enough. He needed to get away, even if it was just for a couple of days, clear his mind of all the crap that was leaving him with a permanent headache. Maybe then, he would be able to see things clearer. His mind made up, he finished the report for his boss he'd been slaving over, trying to find words to explain that yet again, they had come up with absolutely no new leads. Feeling weary beyond belief, he glanced around the office to find himself alone. Damn, he couldn't even recall the others leaving! More convinced than ever that if he didn't get a chance to spend some alone time soon he would crack, he picked up his coat and left the office, looking forward to a couple of days of R&R. After ordering in a pizza for dinner, he rummaged around in his garage, sorting out what gear he needed before bringing everything into the house to have a proper look at it. It wouldn't do to go hiking with a tent or sleeping bag half eaten by mice. Satisfying himself that the gear was still roadworthy, he packed it all away again and then went to his room to fill a backpack with clothes and other stuff he would need. Glancing out the window, he saw with dismay that it had started to snow. Lazy little white flakes were slowly tumbling from the sky. It wasn't a heavy snow fall but still, the idea of taking his tent was a no go. With a sigh, he went back to the living room and pulled up his laptop. He would look for a cabin instead, since freezing to death because he was stupid enough to sleep outside, even in a warm sleeping bag, wasn't on his bucket list. Patapsco Park wasn't far but big enough to find the solitude he craved. This time of year, there wouldn't be many tourists so finding a place to rent would not be a problem. All he needed was to get provisions the following day before he left town. Deciding to start his weekend in style, he got himself a beer from the fridge and found a baseball game on the TV. With a contented sigh, he sat back and already felt himself relax and looking forward to the next few days. Then his phone rang. Picking it up, he looked at the screen, not recognising the number. He debated briefly whether to answer or not, but then thought better of it. With a resigned sigh, he kept his fingers crossed it wasn't work related.

"Green"

"Hello Lucas."

The voice at the other end sent his heart racing.

"Sabrina?" He was stunned.

"How are you Lucas?" Her voice was warm and soft, just as he remembered.

"Good, thank you. A little surprised to hear from you though." He laughed, feeling a little embarrassed at his own words.

"Yeah, I'm sorry about that."

Her voice was light but Lucas got the impression that she too was a little embarrassed.

"I've been so busy, what with my new job and everything."

"You found work, then?" Lucas said. Sitting back on his sofa, he listened as she told him how she'd managed to get a job at Senator Heffner's office. He'd never heard of the guy but was pleased for Sabrina. The job itself was boring, she told him but she was glad to have found a foothold.

"That's great! I'm pleased for you."

Lucas found himself at a sudden loss for words, not something that had happened to him for a very long time. Before he could think of something to say, Sabrina spoke again.

"I know you're probably mad at me for leaving you without saying goodbye, but I just found it too hard, you know?"

Her voice had gone quiet and his heart did a double flip. He hadn't considered her reasons for not waking him before leaving and the thought that she'd found it tough touched him.

"I'm not mad at you." He said softly. "I just wish you'd left me some contact details, that's all."

"I'm sorry!" She whispered, her voice faltering and for a second, Lucas thought she was going to hang up.

"No! Don't be!" He almost stumbled over his words. "I'm glad you called, very glad."

He heard her sigh of relief.

"You don't know what that means to me, Lucas." She paused for a moment. "I've been thinking about you more than I probably should these last few weeks."

Lucas couldn't help the smile appearing at her words but before he could reply, she spoke again.

"I was wondering, if you're not busy this weekend, would you like to meet?"

The unexpected pleasure flooding his system at hearing her invitation took him by surprise. He wondered whether to cancel his trip and spend the weekend with Sabrina instead. Frowning, he was trying to decide. On the one hand, he really wanted to see her again but he was more than aware of the fact that the X murder investigation was taking its toll on him and he really needed a break.

"I'm sorry, Sabrina, but I've got plans for this weekend." Regret tinged his voice.

"Oh!" The disappointment in her voice was evident. "Well, never mind."

"I'm going hiking." He said and then had an idea. "How about you come with me instead?"

The words were out before he had a chance to second guess himself.

"Hiking? In this weather?" She laughed.

"Well, I'm not stupid enough to sleep in a tent so I have rented a cabin." He said with a laugh.

Sabrina was quiet for a long moment.

"I'm sorry, Lucas, I can't. I … I have to feed the neighbour's cat. They're away until after Christmas."

Her words came out in a rush and Lucas had the uncomfortable feeling that she wasn't telling him the truth. Feeling more than a little disappointed, he nodded.

"I understand. Maybe some other time?"

"Okay, that would be lovely."

"If you give me your number, I'll call you when I'm back and we can arrange something, okay?"

He wrote down the number she gave him, pleased to hear that she didn't seem too upset.

"Have a good weekend, Lucas. I'm sorry I can't come with you."

"Yeah, I'm sorry too!" He laughed. "But we'll get together soon and I'm looking forward to that very much."

After saying good bye, Lucas wondered about the real reason why Sabrina hadn't wanted to come with him. Her explanation had rung false and not for the first time, he felt that something was going on with her, but what? Shaking his head, he decided to leave that puzzle for another day. Work permitting, he would see if he was free the following weekend.

Chapter 22

The young woman striding into the lobby of the Four Seasons Hotel exuded confidence, her posture straight and elegant, her business suit very obviously designer made. The large bag hanging from her right shoulder had the emblem of a well-known fashion brand clearly on display and her jewellery, though understated, told of money and success. The concierge cast an appreciative glance over her, noting the long dark braid, carefully styled to look both elegant and business like, completing the picture of a very successful business woman. With a friendly smile on her face, she approached the desk, placing her bag beside her on the counter.

"Good afternoon, Ma'am." The concierge returned her smile. "How may I help you?"

The woman in front of him sighed briefly before putting the smile back on her face. She rummaged in her bag, withdrawing a leather wallet and pulled out ID, holding it out to him.

"I'm Katie Palmer, Mr. Larry Prescot's PA. I booked the Royal suite for him, for two nights." She frowned before continuing.

"Mr. Prescot is delayed so he asked me to come in and check to make sure all is as he requested. You should have an email from me to that effect."

She gazed at him, exasperation at her boss clearly evident in her gorgeous green eyes. He smiled, charmed by her and tapped the keyboard in front of him.

"Ah yes, of course. I have your reservation right here, Miss Palmer. Of course, we do everything we can do make our guests' stay as comfortable as possible and the list of requirements you sent doesn't seem to have caused any issues."

"Oh, that's good." She said, a look of relief on her face as she put a hand on her chest, drawing his eyes to her not inconsiderable cleavage.

Pulling himself upright, he gave a sheepish grin but was relieved when she didn't seem to realise where his eyes had drifted to. Instead, she leaned forward slightly, making it very hard for him to keep his eyes on her lovely face.

"You see," she said so quietly, it was almost a whisper. "Mr. Prescott suffers from OCD. If the rooms are not exactly as he wants them, he's likely to have a fit. Even the slightest difference on how the champagne bottle is placed can cause a massive temper tantrum."

She paused, waiting for him to catch up on what she was saying.

"That's why I normally go ahead and check the room, to try and avoid such a thing from happening."

She shuddered briefly. "It's not pleasant when it happens."

"Of course! I'm sure it must be very difficult." He was pleased as punch to hear his voice come out normal, he'd half expected a squeak, he'd been that distracted by the fabulous swell of her generous breasts!

"The top floor is only accessible with a special elevator key, so I'll get you a key card for the door to the suite and have one of the bell hops escort you."

"That would be marvellous, thank you so much."

The smile she gave him dazed him for a second before he remembered his job, programming the key card and handing it over to her.

"Here you are, Ma'am." he said with his best smile.

"Thank you, that's wonderful. Mr. Prescot is expecting a guest tonight. Could you please ensure the Senator is shown up to the suite as soon as he arrives? He may be here before Mr. Prescot but I'll be on hand to welcome him." She gave him another blinding smile.

"Of course! I'll make a note." He tapped the keyboard again.

They often had prominent people stay at the hotel, quite often politicians or foreign dignitaries, even a film star or two. The hotel was noted for its discreet staff, a very important fact to some of their guests.

"There, that's done. Please don't hesitate to let me know if you need any further assistance."

"Thank you so much. I'll be sure to do that." she replied, giving him a saucy smile.

"In fact, I'm wondering what to do tonight. As you know, Mr. Prescot has an important meeting this evening but he won't need my assistance." She left the unvoiced question lingering and he was quick enough to realise what she was implying.

"As it happens, I finish my shift at seven. I would be happy to show you around, maybe go for a bite to eat somewhere?"

He knew it went against his professional code of conduct to chat up clients but since she wasn't a client, strictly speaking, he thought he could get away with it. Her eyes had widened at his words and she nodded gratefully.

"That would be great, Paul." She said with a glance at the name tag pinned discreetly to his pristine uniform. "I should be free by about eight thirty, if that's not too late?"

"Not at all. I look forward to it."

He gave her another of his winning smiles, pleased with himself. He waved over one of the bell hops and gave him instructions to escort Miss Palmer to the Royal Suite, watching the very delectable sway of her rear as she walked over to the elevators before disappearing from view.

Chapter 23

With a sigh of relief, Sabrina shut the heavy door of the suite after the bell hop had left, a grateful smile on his face at her generous tip. Leaning against the closed door for a moment, Sabrina took a few deep breaths to steady herself. To the right of the entrance hall were steps leading to a huge living room, with doors either side of the large panoramic windows leading out to a fabulous roof terrace. The master bedroom and bathroom where located at the back. She knew all of this without having to investigate, she'd studied the floor plan on the hotels' website, memorising every last detail. Sabrina made her way over to the doors leading to the terrace, blind to the magnificent views, instead, her mind was focused on her preparations. Making sure both doors were locked, she did the same with the dining room door and the door to the study just off the living room. She had a brief glance around the opulent master bedroom and the ensuite bathroom. Both rooms were beautifully appointed, the bathroom outfitted entirely in white marble with gold fittings, thick fluffy towels and matching robes as well as an array of expensive designer cosmetics and bath paraphernalia completing the display of luxury. With a grim smile, she looked at the gorgeous free-standing bath tub. A momentary image of its beautiful white enamel splattered with red blood blurred her vision. Shaking her head to clear the picture from her mind, Sabrina turned and left the bathroom. She wouldn't be needing the tub tonight. Returning to the living room, she glanced at her watch. The Senator would be arriving in a little over an hour, expecting to meet Mr. Larry Prescot, potential donor for future campaigns.

Sabrina knew she had plenty of time to get everything ready, but she felt nervous. Despite knowing that this was going to be her last assignment, she went through the familiar ritual of getting herself ready, sure it would calm her screaming nerves. Carrying her bag into the master bedroom, she slowly undressed, laying her ridiculously expensive suit and the pale pink silk top carefully on the huge bed. She stripped off to her underwear before reaching into the bag, pulling out the bodysuit and slipped it on, the tight fit of the sleek material surrounding her naked skin like a comfort blanket. Once she'd fitted her knife into its usual place, she pulled out several plastic zip ties, some tape and her taser. Double checking that she had everything she needed, she went back into the bathroom and got one of the bath robes, slipping it over her suit. The robe was soft and light weight and, more importantly, long enough to conceal what she was wearing underneath. Since entering the suite, Sabrina hadn't bothered wearing surgical gloves as she usually did but now she shoved a pair into the pocket of her bath robe just because she couldn't stand the thought of getting any of the Senator's blood anywhere on her skin. It was no longer necessary to avoid leaving finger prints or any other forensic evidence, the law enforcement would have all the evidence they could dream of on all of her previous assignments. When she finally heard the knock on the door, she took a deep breath. This was it, ready or not, the only way to go now was forward. She picked up the taser, letting the hand holding it slide into the pocket of her bathrobe, careful to keep her finger off the trigger and went to open the door. Despite the gravity of what was about to happen, the surprised look on the Senator's face almost made her laugh out loud but she managed to keep a welcoming smile on her face. The success of her plan depended on her having the advantage of surprise and she had no intention of squandering that.

***

Senator Steven Heffner sat at his desk, phone in hand, trying not to lose his patience with his new wife.

"I'm really sorry, Whitney, but I can't cancel this meeting!"

How many fucking times did he have to explain? Listening to Whitney whining about not having spent any time together since their honeymoon, he frowned, wondering if he had made a mistake marrying his friend's widow. She was a bit of a pain, sometimes her neediness drove him mad but the lure of her money had been too great. He was more ambitious than ever and going for the top job, he needed money, and lots of it. He knew he could be a contender for the next presidential race, all he needed were additional backers, people with huge wealth and from what Sonia had told him, this Larry Prescot was just what he was looking for. Whitney would just have to suck it up. If he succeeded, he knew she would make an excellent First Lady. She was still a beautiful woman and she knew how to carry herself in public. Along with Rachel, her and Daniel's daughter, they would present the perfect American family to the general public and he knew how important image was.

"I have to go, sweetheart."

He said with a finality in his tone. Apparently, Whitney had heard it too and finally relented.

"I'll make sure we have next weekend together, okay?"

He hung up without waiting for her response and checked his watch. Time to go if he didn't want to be late for his meeting. He called his driver and told him to take the rest of the night off since he planned on driving himself to the Hotel. It wasn't far and sometimes, it was nice to be alone. One way or another, he always had people around him, aides, staff or other members of the Senate and though he loved what he did with a passion, there was the odd moment, like now, when he relished a little solitude. He spent a couple of minutes in the bathroom adjoining his office to make sure his appearance was perfect. He grinned at his own reflection, rubbing his hands in anticipation. He knew he could convince Larry Prescot to back him. His silver tongue and persuasive manner had always served him well in the past, no reason why he shouldn't succeed tonight. With a final glance in the mirror, he collected the keys to his Mercedes, a car he kept at the office for just such occasions, picked up his leather briefcase and left the office. He hit the tail end of DC's evening rush hour and cursed a blue streak, checking his watch frequently to make sure he wasn't going to be late. Finally, with only a few minutes to spare, he pulled up outside the Hotel entrance and handed his keys to the waiting valet, before walking into the lobby. Marble and expensive looking gold fittings along with huge planters gave the place a luxurious feel, it fitted his persona perfectly.

"Good evening, Sir. How may I help you?" The concierge gave him a polite smile as he approached the reception desk.

"I am expected in the Royal Suite." Steven said.

"Yes, of course! We have been informed that you would be arriving, Sir. I'll get a bell hop to accompany you." The concierge said with a smile, obviously having recognised him since he didn't ask his name.

Steven smiled back, pleased with the man's reaction and then followed the bell hop to the elevators, noting that he needed a key to access the top most floor where the Royal Suite was located. Steven was impressed to see that the hotel took appropriate security measures, he had the same kind of security at his apartment building.

"There you are, Sir. Have a good evening." The bell hop pointed at the large door at the end of the corridor and then retreated back into the elevator. Steven walked the few steps to the door, readjusted his tie and knocked. Nobody answered and he was just about to knock again when the door opened and before him stood a beautiful young woman, dressed only in a bathrobe.

Chapter 24

"Good evening, Sir." Sabrina said, a fake smile plastered on her face and then opened the door wider for him to step through.

"Please excuse my get up but Larry has been very naughty and simply couldn't help himself!"

She grinned at the stunned expression on his face, but he stepped through the door past her, allowing her to close it quietly behind him.

"I didn't realise Mr. Prescot had company." The Senator voiced his surprise, turning to look at her.

Sabrina held her breath, wondering whether he was going to recognise her. But he showed no signs of knowing who she was, the lecherous grin on his face making her want to throw up. Sabrina struggled to keep her face blank, the urge to lash out almost overwhelming her. Covertly taking a deep breath, she shrugged her shoulders, then took a step towards him.

"I don't always travel with him but DC has some fabulous shops." She held out a hand, pointing to the right. "If you would like to wait in the sitting room, Larry will be out shortly."

The Senator took one last look at her but then nodded and took the few steps down into the large, opulently decorated living room. Sabrina followed at a safe distance, all of her senses on high alert, watching his every move. He wandered over to the windows and admired the spectacular views.

"Would you like a drink while you wait?" Sabrina asked as she came up behind him, the hand holding the taser ready to slip out of the pocket as soon as he turned towards her.

"That would be ..."

He never got to finish the sentence because Sabrina curled her finger around the tasers' trigger and watched as the metal darts hitting him with unerring accuracy in the centre of his chest. He let out a squeal as the pain hit, twitching and finally crumbling to the floor. She sent another charge through him and watched with cold glee as his body arched before flopping back down again. Once she was sure he was out cold, she shrugged off the cumbersome bathrobe, throwing it carelessly onto one of the huge sofas. She removed the darts from his chest and then proceeded to tie his hands behind his back. She tied his ankles together with another zip tie, using a third one to secure his bound ankles to the heavy coffee table in the living room. He could not be allowed any chance of trying to kick out or get to her in any way. Normally, this wasn't a problem she had to deal with since her targets usually ended up in the bath tub. This time however, she wasn't going to trouble herself with that. It would be hard work trying to drag him through the large suite and hefting him into the beautiful tub. The bathroom was too gorgeous for what she had in mind but more than that, she hoped his blood would stain as much of the expensive fabric as possible. While Sabrina waited for the Senator to regain his senses, she put on the latex gloves, just the thought of actually touching him sent shudders down her spine. But she knew that once she'd started, there was no way of knowing when she'd stop. Seeing him for the first time in ten long years had brought out the very worst in her and she was beyond ready. A sudden image of the day of her mother's funeral invaded her mind and Sabrina remembered, reliving it in horrendous detail.

The church was packed with mourners, most of them Steven's friends and acquaintances. She saw many faces she recognised from the political scene but there seemed to be no one she knew on a more personal level. She sat next to Steven in the front, staring at her mother's ornate casket, the top of it completely covered by floral tributes, too numb to feel anything. Sabrina didn't hear any of the service, it was only as Steven got up to speak that her mind focused. He stood there, lamenting the death of his beloved wife and Sabrina had to take deep breaths to stop herself from vomiting all over the floor.

"Serena was and always will be the light of my life."

He spoke with such sincerity, she could almost have believed his lies, but she knew better. It was because of him that her mother was now dead, he'd turned her into the wreck she'd become with his coldness, his constant demands for Serena to do this and that, be more attentive, be more beautiful, blah blah blah. Sabrina had witnessed more than once the shouting matches, well it was usually Steven doing the shouting while her mother just stood there, taking the verbal abuse with her head bowed. By the end, there had been no fight left in her mother and Sabrina had despised her for it. Finally, the service was over and the congregation followed the coffin out of the church into the cemetery in solemn silence. She stood beside Steven, watching with dry eyes as her mother was lowered into the ground when Steven put his arm around her shoulder, his fingers biting into her tender flesh.

"You better start looking like you're actually sad, you stupid bitch!"

As he whispered into her ear, he increased the pressure on her shoulder and Sabrina felt an intense stab of pain. Her eyes filled with tears as the pain radiated down her arm and she wondered briefly, if he'd actually had managed to break a bone.

"That's better!"

His whispered words sent a shudder down her spine as the silent tears rolled down her cheeks. She was dimly aware of people murmuring, saying what a wonderful man Steven was, caring for his devasted stepdaughter on what must surely be an extraordinarily painful day for the young girl.

With a jolt, she came back to the present and saw that he started to wake up. It took him a moment to figure out what was going on, clearly confused when he realised he couldn't move his arms or legs. He looked up at her.

"What the fuck is going on here? Untie me!"

He sounded weak and Sabrina was glad. She smiled and shook her head.

"I'm afraid I can't do that, Daddy dearest."

At her last words, confusion and disbelief were evident on his face.

"What the hell are you talking about? I'm not your father, you crazy bitch!"

His voice grew a little stronger with his outrage.

Sabrina chuckled at that.

"No, you're not, are you, Steven? Although you certainly knew how to pretend, at least for a little while."

Seeing that he still didn't recognise her made her furious.

"Forgot all about me, have you, you fucking son of a bitch?"

She stood, looking down at him, fury making her eyes glitter. Finally, she saw his eyes widen as he realised who stood in front of him.

"Sabrina?"

His tone told her he had difficulty reconciling her current image with the last one he'd had of her, naked, destroyed, bleeding and half dead.

"The very one!" She replied, her voice cold. "Not quite how you remember me, I guess."

With great satisfaction, she watched as fear flitted across his face.

"I just bet you're wondering what is happening here, aren't you?"

"I don't fucking know what you think you're doing, you crazy bitch but let me tell you, you'll regret it very much!" He actually sounded as if he believed his own words.

Sabrina couldn't help but laugh at his wasted bravado.

"You really think you'll get out of here alive?" Shaking her head, she reached into the pouch and pulled out the knife. "Recognise this?"

His eyes widened as he watched her press the small button, releasing the shiny blade.

"What are you doing with that?"

This time, the fear was evident in his voice, it seemed he finally understood the predicament he was in. Sabrina let her gaze wander over the shiny steel blade, not bothering to look at him as she replied.

"I'm going to kill you with your own knife, Steven."

Her matter of fact tone did not go unnoticed by the man laying on the floor before her.

"You can't do that, you're too much of a coward!"

He spat out at her and just for a second, Sabrina recoiled, memories of past insults threatening to overwhelm her mind before fury at his words fired her blood. She stepped around him and got hold of the zip tie binding his hands, pulling him upright against the sofa. His outraged cries at the pain this must have caused did nothing to soothe her. Ignoring him, she walked over to the table and picked up the tape, pulling a strip off and swiftly covering his mouth with it. She'd acted so fast, Steven didn't realise what she was doing until the tape was firmly covering his mouth. In his new upright position, he had no chance of moving, no way of trying to avoid whatever craziness was coming for him. He noticed that his legs were attached to the heavy table and it finally dawned on him that he was very effectively tied up and unable to move. It suddenly occurred to him that she may well go through with her threat to kill him. That thought made him break out in a cold sweat, the fear rolling through him, making his heart rate speed up. Breathing heavily, he watched as she approached, the knife in her hand glinting in the many little star shaped lights fitted in the ceiling. Helplessly he watched as she brought down the knife and cleanly cut through his shirt but without the blade touching his skin, a fact that told him she had considerable skills using that knife. He moaned at the relief of not having been cut. Sabrina spread his shirt open, exposing his chest, looking at him for a brief moment.

"Do you know what I remember most from our night, Steven?"

Without waiting for an answer, he couldn't have said anything anyway, she touched the tip of the blade to his throat and nicked the skin deeply enough to send a trickle of blood down his neck. It stung a little but nothing he couldn't cope with.

"The marks you left on me that night."

She moved the knife down his chest, cutting across his right nipple, this time applying more pressure. The pain made him moan louder, because that really fucking hurt. Swiftly, she moved down his body, recreating a map of injuries, the same as he had done to her. With each cut, the level of pain increased, the blood flowing more freely now, although nothing life threatening. Steven moaned when she stopped at his waistband, fear of what she was going to do making his eyes water. Calmly, she slid the knife through the fabric of his slacks, cutting away his clothing, leaving only his underwear intact. Another swift flick of the knife and his underwear fell away, exposing him to her cold stare, his dick limp with fear. Sabrina stood looking at it, shaking her head.

"Not such a big man now, are you?"

She leaned a little closer, but not anywhere near close enough for him to get at her. He frantically tried to think of a way of getting away from her or, at the very least, try and lash out somehow but he soon realised that she'd done such a thorough job of tying him up, there was absolutely nothing he could do to defend himself.

"How's the pain? Coping alright?" She gave him a cold look as if to assess her handiwork so far.

"I can see that you are, so let's see how you deal with this."

The next moment, the blade descended, entering his chest just below his ribs, slipping in easily. It wasn't until she twisted it that the pain hit. He cried out, the fiery pain rocketing through his entire body, tears flowing down his cheeks unchecked. He thought he was going to pass out from the intensity of the pain but he wasn't that lucky. The fucking bitch obviously knew what she was doing and despite the pain, he felt fury rise within. It didn't last long though because her arm descended again, this time she pierced the other side, further to the back, the sleek knife penetrating right through to his kidney. Another white-hot pain shot through him and then he did pass out, gratefully sinking into the blackness with a feeling of relief.

The shock of having cold water thrown in his face brought him round again too soon. Sabrina sat on the sofa opposite him, looking at him, waiting. Her cold gaze wondered over his damaged body before she looked up, meeting his eyes.

"You're probably wondering if the wounds will kill you and I can confirm that eventually, they will. But it will take some time and from what I've heard, slowly bleeding to death is extremely painful."

Her monotone voice sent another bolt of mortal fear through him.

"I haven't really got the time or the inclination to wait that long, so we'll speed things up a little, okay?"

She stood and pulled his arms to one side, making him topple over. There was nothing he could do to stop her; the blood loss was already too much and had robbed him of most of his strength. He felt her slice the skin up along from his wrists, realising she was opening his veins just before a new wave of pain hit. He cried out again, although all that could be heard was a muffled sound thanks to the tape covering his mouth. He saw her crouch down next to him, watching his reaction. He could feel the blood flowing faster and she was right, it did hurt. As if she'd read his mind, she nodded with a satisfied look on her face.

"Good."

She reached out and gave him a shove, sending him crashing on his back. The wound in the side of his back sent another wave of pain through him. Kneeling beside him, Sabrina studied him for a moment.

"Nearly done now, Steven." She cast a glance at a mantle clock and nodded. "I guess another half hour or so should do it."

When he moaned at her words, she tutted.

"You know, you could be a little more grateful. I wasn't this considerate with the others!"

Others? She'd killed others? Despite his weakened state, he realised, finally, that it was his fault. All of this, regardless of how many she'd killed before him, he had been the one to set this in motion. That night, he'd enjoyed himself with her but now, as he felt his own death approach, he regretted what he'd done. Not only because she'd come after him and had gotten her revenge but also because he knew that he'd ruined her life. Yet Steven had never given it another thought, his mind focused on getting his career where he wanted it to go, his ruthless ambition driving him forward without a backward glance to the devastation he left behind in his wake.

When he'd come back a few days after he'd had his fun with her, he had been furious to find her gone and angrier still when he'd discovered that she'd taken his money. In his anger, he hadn't realised that the knife was gone too. The first thing he'd done was call Daniel who'd turned up a short while later.

"What the fuck do I do now?" He was furiously pacing around his office, alternatively pulling a hand through his hair and pounding his fists on his desk. "The bitch emptied my safe!"

"Calm the fuck down, Steven!" Daniel's cold tone eased his tension a little.

"Provided she doesn't turn up unexpectedly, we can spin this, no problem."

His friend stared at him pensively, clearly wondering what had provoked Sabrina's flight. Steven avoided his friend's eyes, not wanting to have to say more but Daniel had known him too long to be fooled by him.

"What are you not telling me, Steven? I know there is something else and unless I have all the facts, I can't help."

Steven had been reluctant to tell him at first but then decided he could trust his friend with the truth.

"I had a night of fun with her." He started. "I may have been a little rough but that's all. There was no reason for the crazy bitch to run off like that."

In the end, Daniel had gotten all the sordid details out of him and had sat there, shaking his head.

"You really are stupid ass! You never, ever shit where you eat! Have you not learned that yet?" Daniel yelled as he started pacing the room, shaking his head in disbelief.

"You better hope she doesn't report this! If she does, there will be nothing I can do to help."

Steven blanched at his words. "She wouldn't dare! Who's going to believe her anyway?"

Even to his own ears, he sounded weak and he didn't like it.

"If they do forensic comparisons to the imprints you say left on her, you're fucked, my friend. Did you at least use condoms?"

The look of disbelief on his friends' face as Steven shook his head was evident.

"You really are a stupid son of a bitch!" Daniel said, running a frustrated hand through his thinning hair.

Pacing some more, he took a large gulp of his Scotch.

"You better hope and pray she doesn't go to the Police! We'll wait a few days and if nothing happens, we'll put out a statement about her going off to Europe to finish her schooling. The tragic death of her mother would be too difficult to deal with here so we felt a complete change was the best solution." Steven nodded, hoping his friend was right. If he got away with this, he would be free to continue with his ambitious plans. And he had gotten away with it, until now.

Trying to focus on the woman kneeling beside him, he saw that he'd created a monster. What had seemed a bit of rough fun for him had devasted her, broken her very humanity and he realised that he deserved to die. He wanted to tell her that he was sorry but even without the tape covering his mouth, he doubted that anything he could have said to her would make any difference to the outcome. She was too far gone, he could see the madness in her eyes. Sabrina leaned forward, bringing her face closer to his.

"Are you sorry, Steven? Are you sorry for what you did that night?"

It was uncanny how she knew what he was thinking. With effort, he managed to give a small nod.

"That's good." He could hear the satisfaction in her voice.

"You realise that your regret is worthless, don't you? You are very close to dying now and I will do nothing to stop that from happening. Scum like you don't deserve to live. You drove my mother to her grave, you fucking son of a bitch. For that alone you deserve every last bit of pain I can inflict on you." She raised the blade one last time, slicing across his belly, exposing his entrails.

"Good bye, Daddy dearest." Her whispered words were the last thing Steven Heffner heard before he passed out.

Chapter 25

Sabrina sat on the sofa in her small rented house, staring at the phone in her hand. She'd been dithering for the past half hour, arguing with herself about the pros and cons of making the call. She didn't want to think about what had happened earlier. With every other assignment, she had made it a habit of mentally retaking her steps. It always helped to make sure she hadn't made any errors, had left nothing behind that could be linked back to her. After the first one, she'd struggled for almost a week, her mind a swirl of memories, both of what she'd done and what had been done to her. With every new assignment, she'd learnt to cope better. Perfecting the art of compartmentalising her thoughts and actions was her way of dealing with her feelings, thus enabling her to move forward and keeping nightmares at bay. Grabbing the Tequila out of the fridge, she took a long shot straight from the bottle. It wasn't going to change anything but the alcohol calmed her sufficiently to begin the process. Casting her mind back to earlier in the evening, she replayed events in her mind, a bit like a mental video.

After the final slice of the blade and her whispered good bye, she'd left Steven on the floor of the living room and had gone back to the plush master bedroom, stripped off her suit and changed back into her normal clothes. Folding the bodysuit carefully, she slipped it into a plastic bag and stowed it in her bag. Stepping into the beautiful bathroom, Sabrina reapplied her makeup, making sure she looked perfect again. Glancing at her reflection in the huge bathroom mirror, she stood for long moments, barely recognising the face looking back at her. At a casual glance, she looked perfectly normal, her face betraying none of what she'd just done. Her eyes however were a different matter. Although beautiful, the lush green of the contact lenses vivid in her pale face, there was an emptiness there that hadn't been visible before. Unwilling to deal with the emotions swirling in the depths of her, she checked her watch and realised that she would have to sneak out the back door if she wanted to avoid the concierge from earlier. The poor sap would be waiting for her, wondering why she'd stood him up but Sabrina wasn't inclined to feel any remorse. Without looking at the prone figure laying on the no longer pristine carpet, she walked out of the suite, quietly closing the door behind her. She took the elevator down to the first floor and then exited the building via the staircase, grabbing a cab a block further down to take her home.

She'd gone through her ritual of taking a shower, cleansing herself, ridding herself of the memories. Only this time, it wasn't working. Her mind would not let her forget, nor was she able to push the images invading her mind's eye away. Pacing through the small house, she'd tried to figure out what to do, alternatively taking the Tequila out of the fridge, then putting it back, pulling out her small brown bottle of Valium, only to put it back into her bathroom cabinet. Now she sat looking at the phone, her fingers had dialled the number without her realising and all she needed to do was to press the call button. Refusing to think about it any longer, she touched the button and then raised the phone to her ear.

***

After saying good bye to Lucas, she sat still for a very long time, her mind replaying the conversation over and over. She hadn't thought about what she would say to him and when she'd blurted out her request, she felt mortified. When he said he had other plans, she died a little more inside, knowing that she wouldn't see him again. Remembering how she'd felt as he'd held her no longer had the same effect, she could feel the distance between then and now widening and felt utter desolation. Even his offer to go with him wasn't enough to stop her from sinking deeper into the despair that threatened to drown her and so she had refused, coming up with some stupid excuse about an imaginary cat. Should she have said yes to his offer? Knowing that this would be the last chance she had to spend some time with him, maybe. But since she also knew that lying to herself had to stop, Sabrina was sure that her decision had been the right one. She had done too much, endured too much and had spent the last ten years living a life unimaginable to most people. Knowing there would be no redemption, she'd realised that spending a weekend with Lucas, pretending to be just a regular person would have been beyond her capabilities. Not only that, but she feared that further contact with her would also have done terrible damage to Lucas. Once he found out who she really was, he'd struggle to come to terms with his attraction for her. No, she'd done the right thing by refusing to go with him. But knowing that didn't stop the pain she felt inside. What little humanity was left in her wept for the missed opportunity, even if her eyes remained dry. Her glance fell on the brown envelope sitting on the table in front of her and her breath caught. Fear mingled with a strange sense of calm, the knowledge that what the envelope contained would change her life forever making her senses sway. Of course, she'd known that all along, after all, she'd ordered it for a reason. At the time, she'd thought that it was just in case of emergency. In her efficiency to make sure every angle was covered, she'd also prepared for something going wrong. Killing the Senator had been a risky undertaking and right up until the last moment, just before he'd turned up at the hotel, Sabrina hadn't been sure it would all work out as planned. She hadn't spent as much time on him as she had with the other assignments, leaving some of it to chance, hoping her hastily put together plan wouldn't collapse. In the end, it hadn't been the plan that was the problem. Knowing what she was about to do, she'd felt a tinge of fear, a weird kind of darkness hanging like a cloud over her. She realised now that it was because, unlike any of the others, she knew the Senator, had lived with him for many years and had been shaped and damaged by his actions in a way that was irreparable. Equally, Sabrina accepted that, having carried out her plan, she'd closed the door on any kind of normalcy she may have found. In her mind, anything that had happened before the killing of the Senator had no bearing on the rest of her life, truly believing she could start over somewhere else, free of any kind of stain on her. She'd had enough experience in changing her identity, she could have done it again. But not now. Now, she knew she'd crossed a line. By killing Steven, she'd effectively stopped having a purpose and no matter how screwed up that sounded, it was the truth. All that remained, was to try and do the right thing and put her affairs in order. With a sigh, she grabbed her laptop. Working on autopilot, she started erasing all traces of both Larry Prescot and Katie Palmer. Early morning light filtered through the window as Sabrina saved the last of her work on a USB stick and placed it with the others in the small box sitting beside her on the coffee table. Each had a small label attached to it, with names and dates clearly written on it. Carefully, she placed the lid on the pretty little box, looking at the blue and white pattern that decorated it. It was a gift box and to her, the contents of this box were indeed a gift. Sealing the box with clear tape, she held it for a moment, an intense feeling of sadness flowing through her. Dealing with the Senator had been the hardest thing she'd ever done. Not because he didn't deserve every last stab of pain or the realisation that his death was slowly approaching, nor was it the fact that it had been her who had delivered him to his fate. No, the burden she'd carried for so long should have lifted with him finally out of the way and yet, throughout the whole time, she'd had glimpses of herself as a young girl, happy and carefree, her mother still the loving Mama who had cherished her, who had loved her and who had protected her. But in the end, even her mother had abandoned her, instead turning to a man who would destroy both of their lives and who would ultimately drive her to her death through his ambitious callousness. The whole process of change had started the day her mother had met Steven. She'd always thought that once Steven was dead, she would be free but now she realised, she'd been wrong all these years. Instead, it would end with Sabrina alone, once again unprotected and left to cope on her own. She realised that everything she'd done had been almost predestined, so many *"if onlys"*, so many chances missed to avoid arriving at the point she found herself now. The sadness she felt was for the lost little girl she'd once been, for the lost teenager and finally, the lost woman she'd become. Meeting Lucas, feeling again for the first time in many years had come too late, the damage to her very soul too great to be healed by the possibility of someone else's love. With a sigh, she put the box down.

Chapter 26

Lucas arrived at the park just before noon and once he'd collected the keys to the cabin, put away his groceries and dumped his backpack in one of the two bedrooms. He'd brought along a smaller pack, big enough to hold some provisions to cover a decent hike. He packed a couple of bottles of water, a handful of energy bars and his rain cover. Although the weather had cleared up after the brief snowfall the night before, this time of year, it could change very swiftly. Rain was never too far away but for now, the weak winter sun shone brightly and Lucas was eager to get outside. Out of habit, he picked up his phone and was just about to put it in his pocket when he saw he had no signal. With a grin, he switched it off and dropped it onto the small coffee table. He would enjoy his weekend off the grid, even if, for a moment at least, he wished Sabrina had said yes to his offer. He meant what he'd said to her the night before and he was determined to make good on his promise. He would arrange a weekend in DC, take her to see all the sights, play tourist and generally show her a good time. Right now though, nature was calling and he stepped out of the cabin, locking the door behind him. Breathing in the clean fresh air, he sighed contentedly and started walking.

By late Sunday afternoon, Lucas felt refreshed, his mind clear once again. He packed up his things, stowed what little he had brought with him in the car and made his way back to the city. Once home, he unpacked and then wondered what he should do for dinner. Picking up his phone, he decided to order a take out. He'd completely forgotten that he'd switched off his phone, shaking his head with a grin on his face. Powering up the phone to place his order, the grin vanished when it pinged incessantly with missed calls and countless voice messages. Lucas stared at the phone in his hand in consternation. The noise coming from it had finally stopped and he saw that most of the missed calls were from Dan but there was also one from his boss. An uneasy feeling snaked its way through his mind and with apprehension, he called Dan, not bothering to listen to the many messages.

"What the hell, Lucas! Where have you been?" Dan demanded, sounding stressed.

"I've been out at Patapsco Park for the weekend. What is going on?"

Dan snorted down the phone. "Better put your TV on, pal! We've got victim number 7!"

"Fuck!"

Lucas grabbed his remote and switched the TV to a news channel, sinking down onto his sofa as he watched, a growing sense of horror invading his system. The news reader was talking about the murder of a prominent Senator, found late last night at a posh hotel in downtown DC. The picture switched to the outside of the hotel where a reporter updated the viewing public about the murder.

"Police are still here outside the Four Seasons Hotel where Senator Steven Heffner was found. Forensic teams have been working at the scene since the body was discovered late last night. We have also seen FBI agents entering the building, it would appear that the murder is being handled at the very highest level."

Lucas put the TV on silent, trying to process what he'd just heard.

"Lucas?" Dan was shouting down the phone.

He put the phone back to his ear.

"Sorry, just trying to get my head around this. I take it he's been killed by the woman?"

"Yeah, but this time, she didn't leave her usual mark!"

Dan sounded pissed off and Lucas wasn't sure whether that was because of the absence of the mark or because his phone had been switched off the entire weekend.

"Well, then how do we know it was her?"

"Because of the wounds." Dan said.

"She pretty much used all of her previous moves on him!"

He paused, taking a deep breath before continuing.

"I tell you Lucas, she really went to town on this one. The coroner reckons there are at least ten different stab wounds although he thinks the Senator bled to death like all the others."

It took Lucas a moment to process what Dan had just told him. The one thing that rang clearly through his account of events was that she was starting to fall apart. Mutilating the latest victim in such gruesome fashion was a clear indicator that she'd started to unravel, and Lucas felt afraid of what else was to come. Not only was there a very short period of time between this and the last kill, but the ferocity had increased at an alarming rate. If she was no longer able to control herself, then he feared that they would find a trail of fresh victims in quick succession. They needed to find her and stop her!

"The boss has requested that we go to DC first thing tomorrow. He wants us to liaise with the agents at HQ." Dan said.

"Okay, I'll meet you at the office so I can put together everything we have on our case. Fuck, Dan!" Lucas ran a hand through his hair as he thought about the enormity of what lay ahead.

"Yeah, I hear you." Dan said quietly. "See you tomorrow."

Chapter 27

Sabrina packed the last of her belongings and closed the suitcase with a sigh. Against her better judgement, she'd gone online and had read the news about the Senator's murder. He'd been found late last night, the Police had released a short statement, giving out no further details other than that he'd been murdered and that the FBI was going to be assisting them. She sat back as she absorbed that fact. She hadn't marked the Senator like she had all the others. Would they make the connection to her previous assignments? She thought that they might and knew she needed to move on quickly. Although she'd worn the bodysuit, she hadn't bothered wiping down anything in the suite so they would find her prints all over the place. As part of her preparation, she had verified that the hotel had security cameras, particularly in the reception area. As far as she had been able to tell, the top floor, where the Royal Suite was located, had none. It had been ridiculously easy to hack into the system to create a malfunction of the system whilst she was in the lobby, so there would be no footage of her. Sabrina knew she wasn't listed on any databases, clearly remembering the thrill of hacking into law enforcement systems to check. The only witness who could describe her in detail was the concierge. That could be a problem because he would remember her alright. She'd always worked on the assumption that the law enforcement agencies would be looking for a male killer. Research she'd carried out had told her that the majority of serial killers were male. This gave her an added layer of cover but now, that advantage was lost. Unsure how long it would be before they put out a picture to the media, she knew she needed to change her appearance once again. She had plenty of options since she'd kept one or two of her previous identities, she just needed to decide which one to use. The thought of becoming yet another person didn't appeal to her. It bothered her that with every change she made, she seemed to lose a little more of her original self and that frightened her.

With a resigned sigh, she looked around the small house she'd been in only a short while. It was a nice place and Sabrina had felt comfortable here. It was the sort of house a small family would have. The thought flashed in her mind, and just for a moment, she let herself imagine what that would feel like. To greet a husband when he came home after a days' work, holding a toddler out to him for a kiss. Shaking her head, she scolded herself. There was no point thinking about such things, they were never meant for her. Picking up the first of the suitcases, she went into the garage and started loading the car. Despite feeling the need to run, Sabrina was reluctant to leave, her emotions running from one direction to another, leaving her confused and scared. Maybe she would put off leaving until the next day. She needed to go out and get supplies if she wanted to change her appearance but she would wait until night fall. This way, it was less likely anyone would see her. It was well after midnight when she finally ventured out, making only one stop at an all-night pharmacy.

For the past seven years, her hair had been all different sorts of colours, ranging from dark brown to red but never had she gone back to her original blonde. After the first assignment had been complete, she was in such turmoil, she had needed a complete change and ever since, going back to her real colour hadn't been something she'd wanted to do. Now though, she felt a strong urge to become herself again, she needed to be able to recognise herself when she looked in the mirror. Now, as Sabrina stood in front of the bathroom mirror, staring at her reflection, she felt better than she had in a long time. For a brief moment, her face morphed into that of her mother when she'd been young. Memories of her Mama surfaced, the two of them standing in front of the mirror in their bathroom, trying out different hairstyles, her mother often doing Sabrina's hair the same way as her own. Mama had once told her that one day, when Sabrina was older, people would think they were sisters instead of mother and daughter. She hadn't exactly understood what her Mama had meant but the brilliant smile on her mother's face was enough for her. If Mama was happy about that, she would be too.

Early next morning, after a restless few hours of sleep, she cast a final glance around the house, having made sure everything was locked and secure. Satisfied, she shut the door and got in her car, waiting for the garage door to open. It would close automatically once she'd left, they house keys were left on the side bench running along one wall. At least the house would be safe.

Unsure where to go next, she headed out of DC and then took the highway south. She'd never been to Florida so this was as good a place as any to head for. The lack of sleep from the past few days finally caught up with her some hours later. Her head hurt and concentrating on navigating the traffic on the busy highway was becoming increasingly difficult. Sabrina found a cheap motel on the way and decided to stop for the night, picking up a pizza to eat in her room. Exhausted, she managed to eat only a small slice of the pizza before she was forced to admit defeat and stretch out on the bed, sleep claiming her as soon as she closed her eyes. It was still dark when she woke up and since she still hadn't found her appetite, she packed her few belongings. Slipping out of the motel unseen, she continued her way south. It was late by the time she crossed into the Sunshine state and after having driven through a small beach town just after Jacksonville, she found an Inn with vacancies. The Inn was run by a surly older woman who informed her that all rooms were non-smoking and breakfast would be served between seven and nine. Sabrina thought her demeanour could do with a bit of work but thanked her politely nonetheless, not wanting to draw undue attention to herself. Even with her changed appearance, she wasn't going to do or say anything that could be recalled easily enough should the right questions be asked. She had a feeling that not much passed the old woman by and that her faculties were in no way diminished by her advancing years. Grimacing at her own paranoia, she let herself into the room, dumping her small suitcase on the bed. It was a nice enough space, a little old fashioned perhaps but it was clean and it would do for one night. While eating a bar of chocolate she'd purchased on her last fuel stop, Sabrina grabbed her laptop and pulled up a map of Florida. Where should she go? The Keys looked appealing but were too crowded for her liking. This time of year, so close to Christmas, the towns would be rammed with mostly retired couples, enjoying the warm temperatures the location offered. Instead, she searched for quieter places, somewhere not too remote but equally not as busy. It was easier to lose yourself in large crowded places but Sabrina couldn't face the thought of being surrounded by thousands of people. She needed some space, needed to rest and figure out what she was going to do next. Not having a plan for the first time in almost ten years unsettled her but she knew one thing with absolute clarity. She would not kill again. The death of the Senator had marked a definite end to her previous existence, now all she needed to do was figure out a plan for her new future.

Chapter 28

It was late morning by the time Lucas and Dan arrived in DC, the traffic a complete nightmare, both out of Baltimore and worse still, getting into Washington. Having parked up, they were greeted at the reception by Special Agent in Charge Tom McClean.

"Gentlemen, nice to meet you, even under these circumstances."

He smiled as they shook hands. He led the way to a suite of offices a couple of floors up, the large open plan design was filled with people, all busy with one thing or another. Tom pointed to a side office where a couple of people were sat, discussing papers before them. Gesturing for Lucas and Dan to enter, he cleared his throat and immediately, the room went quiet, the two men and one woman looking over at them with interest.

"Guys, these are Special Agents Lucas Green and Dan Mortimer from the Baltimore office."

He introduced the three people and then went and sat at the head of the table.

"Have a seat and we'll get started." Tom waited for everyone to get comfortable and then looked over at Lucas and Dan. He handed them a file, explaining as they opened it.

"What we have so far is this. Senator Heffner was due to meet with a potential backer for his next campaign. Initial contact was made via email to his office. We've spoken to his secretary."

He paused for a moment to check his own file.

"Ah, yes, here it is. Sonia Whitmore has been the Senator's secretary for the past seven years. She did a background check on this Larry Prescot. Apparently, it all seemed legit so when

Mr. Prescot requested a private meeting, the Senator agreed. It was set up for Friday night at the Four Seasons Hotel."

Lucas listened, astonished at the length the killer had gone to to get the Senator alone.

"Have you managed to speak to this Larry Prescot?" He asked.

"He doesn't exist!" Jack, one of the other agents replied and Lucas looked at him in shock.

"What?"

Jack nodded, a grim look on his face.

"We searched all available databases. There is no such person, at least not a super-rich legal arms dealer looking to back a potential presidential candidate."

Lucas couldn't believe what he was hearing! Who was this woman who had evaded law enforcement agencies for the past eight years, who killed without leaving a single usable trace?

"But how is that possible?" Dan said, outraged. "You said the Senator's secretary ran checks on this guy!"

"If the killer is as smart as we think she is, it would be relatively easy for her to set up a background for this Larry Prescot." Tom leaned towards Dan.

"Think about it for a minute. Here you are, secretary to a successful Senator, a guy who is looking to go for the top job. We all know just how much a presidential campaign costs, and if you don't, I can tell you it runs into millions of dollars. So now she's got a potential backer, a rich one at that. She does a background check but how deep does she go? She comes across a website detailing the dealings of a certain Mr. Larry Prescot, his connections to the NRA, his willingness to meet with the Senator and Bingo! Same with the Senator himself. He relies on her advice and agrees to the private meeting, thinking now useful such a man could be to his ambitious plans."

Tom paused, waiting for Dan to absorb what he was saying.

"I think she knew him." Lucas said into the quiet room and all eyes turned to him. Tom raised his eyebrows in question.

"How do you figure that out?"

Lucas thought about how to word this, still trying to arrange things in his mind. Leaning on his elbows, he looked at the rest of the group.

"Because she must have known that the money would have been irresistible to Heffner. If she didn't have insider knowledge, how would she have known that her relatively simple ruse would work? I did a little digging on the Senator last night. His first wife was rich and he married her at the time of his first run for Senate. She died a few years later and now, he's just married another very rich woman. He's going for the top job, he needs money and lots of it. So, if you know that he's ambitious enough to maybe overlook certain things in order to get where he wants to go, it stands to reason that maybe he wouldn't look a gift horse too closely in the mouth."

Lucas sat back and watched the others.

"So, I think she must have known him and his ruthlessness to get to the top. And she used that knowledge to lure him to the Hotel."

Tom looked at Lucas, nodding his head, his eyes showing understanding at Lucas's reasoning.

"Makes sense, I guess. But how does that connect her to the other murders? As far as we know right now, the Senator wasn't a paedophile, so why go after him?"

"Yeah, that's what I can't figure out either!" Lucas had to admit. "Are the wounds on the Senator coincidental, meaning someone else killed him or are we looking at the same woman for all the killings? The Senator didn't have the X on his chest, but what are the chances that another killer would use the same methods to kill him? As far as I'm aware, no details regarding the stab wounds on any of the victims were ever released."

"The press knew about the mark she left on all of her victims, hence the nickname." Sara said. "Maybe someone let slip more information?"

Tom nodded. "It could be, but I doubt it."

He sat for a moment, fingers tapping on the table.

"The coroner is doing the autopsy today, once we have his report, we may be better able to judge whether we're talking copycat or if it was the same killer. Let's leave that for a moment and move on, okay?"

Referring to his notes, he continued with the recap.

"According to the concierge at the hotel, a woman came by about an hour before the Senator was due to arrive, claiming to be Mr. Prescot's PA and gained access to the Royal Suite by saying her boss suffered from OCD and she needed to ensure everything was in order. Not thinking anything of it, the concierge handed over a key."

"That's right." Jack interjected. "When I spoke to him, he said she was very convincing, so much so that he never even checked her ID."

Lucas looked at him in astonishment.

"You're telling me he let some woman get access to the most expensive suite in the entire hotel without asking for ID?"

Jack nodded and grinned. "Yeah! By all accounts, she was a looker and had promised to meet him later for a night out."

Lucas shook his head. "I hope he gets the sack, the stupid dick!"

"Oh, believe me, he was quacking in his boots when I spoke to him." Jack grinned again.

"Not only is it against company policy to chat up guests but he also screwed up big time by not checking her ID. Last I heard, he was having a chat with his boss." He rifled through his notes.

"Couldn't even remember her last name, but she called herself Katie. Let's just hope his memory is good enough to recall what she looked like."

"Damn, but she really is a pro at this!" Lucas muttered, trying to get his head around all this new information.

"Does the hotel not have surveillance?" Dan asked.

Tom smiled grimly and nodded. "They do! But, as luck would have it, there was a very convenient computer glitch around about the time the woman turned up so, we have no footage of her."

"A computer glitch? You mean to tell me she disabled the security system on purpose?"

Lucas was getting madder by the minute. Who were they dealing with, Super woman?

Tom gave him a look of astonishment.

"Damn, I didn't make that connection!" He turned to Sara.

"Check out the system at the hotel and see if it was tampered with." Sara nodded wordlessly and pulled up her laptop.

"If anyone can spot interference, Sara can."

The woman smiled at his words but didn't look up from her screen, her fingers flying over the keyboard.

Dan cursed under his breath. "What about the corridor outside the suite?"

Tom shook his head. "According to the hotel, the Royal Suite takes up the whole of the top floor and since it often hosts prominent people who bring their own security, cameras are not installed."

"What the hell?" This time, Dan didn't hide his frustration.

"She had all angles covered." Tom said, his own frustration evident.

"This is a highly intelligent woman, meticulous to a fault and deadly!"

Lucas couldn't have agreed more. He'd thought exactly that himself.

"So, the concierge, can he give us a description?"

"He is doing that as we speak." Tom said. "He's with the sketch artist now. With a bit of luck, it'll match the description you got from your case."

"I'm sorry, Sir." The third agent, Tom had introduced him as Nick, spoke clearly but quietly.

"During the initial interview, he said the woman had dark hair, not red."

"Yeah, I know that." Tom replied. "But you know as well as I do that appearances can be changed, particularly such a simple thing like hair colour."

Nick nodded, his pale cheeks reddening at the slight rebuke.

"Either way, we should have a picture by the end of the afternoon. Until then, let's compare the other similarities." Tom turned to Dan. "You said that some of the injuries inflicted on the Senator match those found on previous victims?"

Dan nodded. "Yes, the stab wound to the liver, for example, has been used on two other victims. The slash across the stomach was found on one other. Also, the slit wrists, she's used that on victim number three." He stopped and swallowed, taking a deep breath before he continued.

"I find it incredibly difficult to understand how you can do that to another human being. It really makes me sick!"

Lucas put a hand on his partner's arm, understanding what Dan was saying. Despite years of dealing with all kinds of horrific scenes of crime, it was difficult to get used to knowing that there were people out there who were capable of such things.

"We also have some prints from the bathroom that don't belong to any of the staff who had access to the suite." Tom said. "We ran them through all data bases and came up with nothing."

"Yeah, that figures!" Lucas grumbled and voiced his earlier musings. "Who is she? Super woman or a freaking ghost?"

Despite the gravity of the situation, his outburst provoked laughter around the table. A knock on the door silenced them as a young man opened the door, carrying trays of sandwiches.

"Sorry Sir, but the lunch you ordered has arrived."

Tom smiled and thanked him. Along with sandwiches, coffee and bottles of water were brought in and Lucas realised he was starving.

"Let's have something to eat. Don't know about you but I need a break!"

Tom grinned at them and reached for a sandwich. Apart from Sara, who was furiously typing away, they all helped themselves to food, the atmosphere in the room still subdued.

"Found it!" Sara said, her voice triumphant.

Every pair of eyes in the room turned to her.

"So, without boring you with the jargon, she put a timer on the bug she planted."

Dan looked at her in total astonishment. "Say that again?"

Sara shrugged. "This woman knows her way around computers, that's a fact. She infected the system with a tiny bug, one that would be spotted fairly quickly by the Hotel's fire walls but not quick enough to prevent the system for malfunctioning for about fifteen minutes. Plenty of time to get what she needed, particularly with a concierge who was thinking with the wrong head."

The last came out with a grin and the men laughed at her dry comment.

"Great work as always, Sara. Thank you. Now eat something!" Tom said and gave her a grateful smile.

Finishing the last of their meal, they were just about to get back to discussing the investigation when Sara's laptop pinged.

"Sir, we've got a picture from the sketch artist." She waited for the file to down load and then turned her screen for the others to see.

Lucas stared at the face and felt his heart stop. If he hadn't already been seated, he would have face planted in total shock, for the face staring back at him was none other than Sabrina.

"Fuck!" His exclamation made everyone turn to him.

"Lucas?" Tom's voice sounded distant as Lucas tried to recover from what he'd just seen. All the pieces of the puzzle fitted together too neatly, he could finally see the almost completed picture and he felt sick. A hand on his shoulder, squeezing hard, brought him back to the present.

"What is going on?"

Tom's voice had lost any trace of warmth. Lucas rubbed a hand over his face, unable to comprehend the full nature of what he knew to be true. He knew he would have to tell them but first, he needed a minute to gather himself. Sighing, he took a breath.

"I know her." His statement hung in the air, the incredulous look on everyone's face testimony to the shock his three simple words had caused.

Chapter 29

After a night of disturbed sleep, Sabrina got up and repacked her case. Claiming to be too busy to have breakfast, she paid the woman for the room and then left, heading south again but still unsure of where exactly she was going. The nightmares that had plagued her were hard to push from her mind, even in the bright sunshine. Her mind was a swirl of images and memories, she could barely concentrate on keeping the car on the road. Finally, she saw a small rest stop coming up and pulled over, switching off the engine with shaking fingers. Staring blankly at the beautiful surroundings, she tried to get some sort of control over her confused and freaked out mind. Opening the car window, she sat and listened for a long time, hearing the waves gently washing against the beach, the sound of seagulls providing a squawking sound track. The air coming in through the open window was fresh and carried a hint of salt, unlocking a memory from long ago, when she'd been small and her Mama had surprised her with an impromptu holiday, telling her what fun they would have whilst they packed their suitcases. They had spent a glorious week at a place very similar to this one, playing on the beach every day, having picknicks in the sand dunes and collecting shells along the long sandy beaches. On the last night, Mama had made a small fire on the beach, telling Sabrina that no holiday by the sea should end without spending an evening on the beach, toasting marshmallows and eating hot dogs. She could still recall the smells and sounds of that night and felt a pain so intense, she thought she might be having a heart attack. Her breath came out fast, her heart beating a rapid tattoo in her chest. Sabrina felt a darkness descending, just as she had when she'd been in the Hotel, waiting for the Senator to arrive. But this time, it enveloped her completely, her mind a swirl of incoherent bits and pieces. Desperately trying to get a grip on her sanity by filling her lungs with deep breaths of the salty air, she fought to regain the upper hand on the desolation that threatened to overwhelm her. She didn't know how long she'd been sat there, fighting to stay in the present but the sun was making its way down towards the horizon, casting rays of brilliant shades of orange across the now still waters, dark ominous clouds gathering at a fast pace. Fascinated, she watched the billowing grey wall approach, impressed by its speed. Despite her fractured mind, Sabrina knew she needed to find somewhere to stay before the storm broke and started the car, driving along the deserted roads, looking for a place to spend the night. She knew she wouldn't be able to sleep despite the bone deep weariness that had invaded her but equally, she didn't think she was capable of driving through the night on unfamiliar roads. Heavy drops of water began splashing down on her windshield, increasing with every second, until she could barely see the road despite her wipers working overtime. Relieved when she spotted a sign a few miles later, she pulled into the small parking area and switched off the engine, listening to steady beat of the rain on her car roof. Sitting in the car for a moment longer, hoping the rain would ease off a little, she flipped down the visor and took in her appearance in the small mirror. Dark circles cast shadows on her pale face, the eyes staring back at her, empty of any kind of emotion. She flipped the visor up again, unable to look at herself any longer. Getting out of the car even though the rain was still falling pretty hard, she pulled her small case from the trunk and ran over to the motel entrance. Even just that short distance left her soaked, her hair sticking to her head, dripping down the back of her neck in an unpleasant manner. The clerk behind the counter made no comment regarding her appearance, his attention focused on the football game playing on the small TV on his desk. In return for her money, he handed her a key, telling her that breakfast wasn't available the following morning as the cook had left for the holidays. She acknowledged his comment with a polite thank you and then went to find her room. Not as clean as the one she'd stayed the previous night, Sabrina took a look around, poking her head into the tiny bathroom. It would do. Grabbing one of the thin towels from the bathroom, she rubbed her hair, trying to get as much water out of it as she could. She pulled out dry clothes and got changed, hanging the wet clothes she'd just taken off on the rail in the bathroom in the vain hope that they might dry overnight. Not bothering to unpack, she stretched out on the bed, the nylon bed cover smelling a little unpleasant, but her mind was occupied with other things. Sabrina stared up at the grubby ceiling as she finally acknowledged the truth. Laying on a cheap bed in a cheap motel, she knew with absolute certainty that she was fast approaching the end. Her mind was collapsing under the weight of her actions, she'd taken so many lives, had deceived, lied and cheated her way through the past ten years. Her justifications for what she'd been doing were being swept away like sandcastles in the rising tide. Sabrina had always thought of the Senator as a monster but now, she saw clearly that she was much worse than him. Blaming Steven Heffner for what she'd done during the last seven years was just a convenient excuse. She could have sought help, could have made attempts to recover from her ordeal. She knew very well that other people had suffered much worse than her and had managed to work through it, building a new life for themselves. But instead, she'd let it fester inside, allowing it to create the monster she had become. In two days' time, it would be the tenth anniversary of Steven's attack, a significant fact that was not lost on her. A wave of tiredness swept through her and closing her eyes, she finally gave up her fight and let sleep invade her disturbed mind. But instead of once again being plagued by nightmares, Sabrina dreamt of her mother. Her dreams were not of the woman her mother had become after marrying the Senator but her sweet, loving Mama. Echoes of childhood laughter rang through her sleeping mind, images of happy times spent at her old home. She saw a younger version of herself sitting in the kitchen, eating cookies still warm from the oven, helping Joshua cleaning the stables and riding through the meadows with Daisy. Those happy memories replaced the horrors from the previous nights. When Sabrina woke the next day, Christmas Eve, she felt more refreshed than she had in a long time. Along with a clearer mind came understanding, her mind filled with calm acceptance as she finally realised where she needed to go. She got her laptop out and went online, looking to put in place her plans to travel, booking a flight out of Orlando for the day after Christmas. Gathering her belongings, she headed out to the car park, stowed away her case and headed back to the main road, making her way to Orlando. This time though, she took her time, enjoying the scenery along the way, winding her window down and letting the breeze blow through her hair. After the storm, the air had a fresh scent although the glimpses she had of the beach running alongside the road showed the debris that had been washed up during the night, bits of driftwood littered the long stretches of golden sand. As she approached the city limits, she headed towards the airport. Sabrina had found a Hotel with vacancies close by when she'd booked her flight and found the allocated parking spaces after doing several tours of the vast, long term parking area. Checking in took a matter of minutes, all she'd taken from her car was the small case and her laptop. She planned on spending Christmas day watching old movies and making good use of room service. She didn't want to go out and see thousands of people having fun, enjoying Christmas with their families. Distracting herself was vital, she didn't want to think about the following day but at the same time, she couldn't face being presented with pictures of happy families. The next morning, she ordered breakfast and then repacked her case. The hotel provided a free shuttle service to the departure hall and Sabrina didn't have to wait long for its arrival. There were several other passengers, many with several suitcases so Sabrina stood, one hand on the handle of her small case, the other hanging on to the vertical handrail as the shuttle sped towards the airport. She was first out once the shuttle had come to a stop and, checking to make sure that the little gift box, now wrapped ready for posting was in her bag, she walked around the departure hall, looking for an open Express Courier Service desk. She filled in the necessary paperwork to have the small package shipped for same day delivery to its destination and paid the fee in cash. With a sigh, Sabrina grabbed what little luggage she had with her and went to check in, handing over her fake ID to the smiling woman at the airline counter. Getting through security took forever, hordes of tourists clogging up every available space and Sabrina breathed a sigh of relief when she finally got to the gate allocated to her flight with barely forty minutes to spare. She took a seat as she waited for the gate to open and embarkation to start. Glancing at the empty seat beside her, she spied a newspaper from the day before and picked it up. As expected, the headline was all about the murdered Senator and Sabrina couldn't help herself. She read the article with interest, shaking her head at the wild speculations as to who had done away with the Senator and the possible reasons why. Everything from a political assassination to an extra marital bit of fun gone wrong was mentioned, although none of the offered choices came even close to the truth. The article finished by stating that the FBI was taking over the investigation since Senator Heffner had been a very prominent figure. She'd known that this would happen and her thoughts briefly went to Lucas. Had he heard about the murder? Surely, he would have by now. He'd told her he would be away for two days, not an entire week so that would mean he'd be back at work today. Sabrina didn't know if he would realise the connection between this murder and all the others. Really, the only thing linking them was the nature of the way she'd killed him, having used several of her previous methods to despatch him. Lucas was an intelligent man and, she suspected, very good at his job, so he would see the similarities and get involved in this latest killing too. Either way, by tomorrow, he would know the full truth about her. She owed him that much at least and had made sure he would be the first person to get his hands on her account of all her assignments. The package she'd posted earlier contained all the information he would need to close all seven cases. She hoped it would be enough.

Chapter 30

All eyes were on Lucas, the shock at hearing those three words evident on all of their faces. Where to start, Lucas thought, desperately trying to hold onto his sanity. What sort of a man was he, almost falling for a serial killer? Worse still, he'd thought she was shy and a little naïve. Had she played him, knowing he worked for the FBI? He recalled telling her about the X murder investigation during their first meeting. But the more he thought about it, the more he knew that couldn't be right, because now he understood why, shortly after him telling her what he did for a living, she'd bolted as if the devil himself was after her. Understandable to be sure, but then why had she contacted him again? Why had she spent the night in his bed, leaving that note? He felt himself go pale when he realised she'd called him shortly after killing the Senator! He had heard in her voice that something wasn't right with her but this?

"Lucas!"

Tom's sharp voice brought him back to the present. He looked at the man, seeing for the first time since meeting him earlier why he was in charge around here. The look on Tom's face had gone from work colleague to interrogator and Lucas felt a sliver of unease.

"Sorry!"

He sighed, knowing that he would have to tell them everything, right from that moment he set eyes on her for the first time, right up to the call on Friday night. Rubbing a weary hand through his hair, he gathered his thoughts and began.

"I know this woman as Sabrina. I met her about two months ago, several weeks into the investigation of the Baltimore case."

Tom put up his hand. "Stop right there, Agent Green. We'll do this by the book."

He gathered his papers and stood, casting a long pensive glance at Lucas, who returned his gaze with a tired nod. Dan sat next to him, a look of total disbelief and shock on his face. Lucas looked at him, unable to speak and got up to follow Tom out of the office.

Half an hour later, they sat in an interrogation room, complete with surveillance and one-way mirror. Just like in the movies, Lucas thought but there was no humour in that. This was real alright; his life and his job were on the line and he couldn't quite see how this was going to play out for him.

"Okay, Agent Green. Let's start at the beginning." Tom's voice was cool and professional, helping Lucas focus on what he had to do.

"As I said, I met her in the bar of a Hotel in Baltimore. I'd gone for a drink after work." He retold the events, trying to remember as many details as he could. Tom didn't interrupt, he sat opposite Lucas, listening and observing.

"I was very surprised to hear from her again some weeks later. She said she wanted to make it up to me and asked if we could meet for dinner. We met at a restaurant near to my house."

He paused for a moment, wondering whether she'd checked him out and had chosen the place on purpose. But to what end? Had she already decided that, if he was willing, and let's face it, he didn't exactly put up a fight when it came to it, that she would go home with him?

"During the meal, did she ask about the investigation?" Tom said.

"No, not at all. In fact …"

Lucas felt the blood drain from his face, cursing at the thought that he really hadn't connected even the most basic dots! Maybe he really was in the wrong job if a pretty woman could make him forget everything he'd learned at the academy.

"What? What have you remembered?" Tom's voice was once again sharp.

"She told me she was moving to DC and that she was looking to get a job at a Senator's office." He rubbed his forehead. "During our last call, she actually told me she was working for Senator Heffner!"

Tom shuffled through his papers until he came to what he was looking for.

"According to the list of names of staff we were given by the Senator's secretary, there was no one called Sabrina on the payroll." He glanced down again.

"The only recent addition to the team, apart from some temp workers was a Katie Palmer." Tom looked at Lucas and then cursed.

"Shit, the woman at the Hotel said her name was Katie! Damn it, it was her, I'm sure! That would make sense and you said yourself that you thought she knew him somehow."

Tom sat back, both men stunned by this new discovery. Tom pressed the button of the intercom.

"Jack, go and show Sonia Whitmore the picture and see if she knows her. I want to know as soon as you do what she says." He turned to Lucas. "Might as well carry on here while we wait."

When Lucas got to the point of his second meeting with Sabrina, he hesitated. As an agent, he knew he couldn't and shouldn't leave anything out but as a man, he was reluctant to spell out what had happened that night.

"After dinner, we went back to my house." He said, waiting for Tom to ask the question he was dreading. He didn't have to wait long.

"Did she spend the night, Agent Green?"

Lucas nodded, hoping he wouldn't be expected to recount the details of what happened in his bed. Tom looked at him for a moment and Lucas saw that he understood.

"What time did she leave?"

Lucas let out a quiet breath. "I don't know. When I woke up, she was gone."

"What time was that?"

"About six thirty. I got ready for work and found a note from Sabrina in the kitchen."

"What did the note say?" Tom's voice was quiet but Lucas was left in no doubt that he would have to reply.

"She thanked me for giving her the best night of her life." He said through gritted teeth, wondering whether any of it had actually been true.

"Do you still have the note?"

Wordlessly, Lucas pulled out his wallet and extracted the small piece of paper, pushing it over to the man across the table. He felt embarrassed at having kept the note like some love-sick teenager, but he'd not been able to bring himself to throw it away. Tom looked at it briefly without touching it.

"We'll have to check this for prints." He looked at Lucas, who nodded.

He knew that, just as he knew that if any prints were found on the note, they would match the ones found in the suite.

"Okay, then what happened?" Tom asked, his gaze once again on Lucas.

"I didn't hear from her again until last Friday night."

Tom sat up a little straighter.

"I was getting ready to have a couple of days away when she called." Lucas said. "She wanted to meet up that weekend but since I'd already made plans, I told her I couldn't. Instead, I asked her if she wanted to come hiking with me. She refused, said she was looking after the neighbour's cat and couldn't leave. We agreed to meet up at a later date." A cold shiver ran down his spine as he realised that Sabrina had called him after killing the Senator.

He stopped and put his head back. He felt exhausted. Retelling what had gone on between him and Sabrina had been hard, a sense of loss at what could have been invaded his mind which made no sense to his logical side. How could he hanker after a serial killer? But no matter how many times he asked himself this very question, all he could see was the young woman who had affected him so deeply, a woman he could have fallen for. That fact he kept to himself and no one was ever going to hear just how deceived he felt, not to mention the fact that he mourned a girl who didn't exist, apart from in his mind.

"Okay, we'll wrap this up for now, Lucas. I don't need to tell you that you're off the case." Tom's voice held a trace of sympathy. "I suggest you go home."

Lucas got up and followed Tom out of the room, not knowing how to feel. His mind was in a whirl, still trying to grasp what had just happened. Dan was waiting for him in the lobby, the look on his face one of sympathy and shock. Lucas stood, looking at his partner and couldn't find a single thing to say.

"I'll be in touch." Tom said with a nod and then turned and left the two men standing there, neither knowing what to say.

"Come on, let's go home." Dan said quietly.

Lucas handed him the keys to their car. "Mind driving?"

Shaking his head, Dan took the keys and started towards the door, Lucas trailing behind. For the first half hour of the drive, neither spoke. Lucas was lost in thoughts, staring out the window with unseeing eyes.

"I don't know what to say to you, Lucas."

Dan finally broke the silence as they approached the Baltimore city limits. Lucas turned to him, watching his friend and partner's profile.

"And I don't know what to tell you, Dan. I'm off the case, obviously and maybe it would be better if we didn't talk about it."

Dan nodded and for the rest of the journey, he remained silent. Pulling up in front of Lucas's house, he turned and looked at him. Lucas held up a hand, indicating that there was nothing to say. With a parting nod, he got out of the car and shut the door behind him, not turning around as he heard Dan pull away.

Chapter 31

Lucas spent a restless night tossing and turning, his mind on a continuous loop of jumbled up memories. Memories of Sabrina in his bed, remembered images of the crime scene photos he'd seen, bits and pieces of conversations he'd had with her. In the end, he got up, unable to stand laying in bed any longer. It was still dark outside as he made his way into the kitchen. Looking out the window into his next-door neighbour's garden, he realised that today was Christmas! The lights twinkling covering the house next to his made him feel lonely for the first time in a very long time. Where was Sabrina now? Lucas cursed, mad at himself for still thinking of her. He needed to see her for what she was. A cold-blooded killer, not some young innocent woman who was all alone in the world, just like him! She was probably out there somewhere, seeking out her next victim while he sat here, worrying about her. He needed to get his act together, for Fuck's sake! He poured himself another cup of coffee and went into the living room, switching on the TV. He was determined to find something to distract him from going completely nuts and for a time, he managed to do just that. Around lunch time, his phone rang and Lucas jumped up, grabbing it in the ridiculous hope that it might be Sabrina. Of course, it wasn't because Lucas recognised the number.

"Hey!" He tried to sound upbeat and failed miserably.

"Lucas, how are you doing?" Dans voice was full of concern.

Lucas didn't know what to say so he didn't respond.

"Listen, Marie and I would like to invite you for Christmas dinner. Might do you good to get out a little, you know?"

Lucas was touched by the offer but knew he couldn't accept.

"That's very kind, Dan, thank you. I wouldn't be very good company though so ..." He trailed off lamely.

"But it's Christmas! You shouldn't be on your own, not today!" Dan said, his tone suddenly firmer.

"I'll be round in about half an hour so get your ass showered and be ready."

Without waiting for a reply, he hung up, leaving Lucas to stare at the phone in his hand. Well, damn! A reluctant grin spread across his face as he went and showered and by the time Dan pulled up outside, he was ready. With a grin on his face, Dan pushed open the car door.

"Get in, it's freezing!"

Lucas couldn't help the answering grin spreading over his own face. It felt good to know that Dan was still willing to spend time with him, knowing that his partner would stand by his side made him feel a lot better.

"I haven't got anything to give to your wife or your kids!" He said. "I completely forgot it was Christmas day!" He sent a sheepish grin in his partner's direction who waved a hand at him.

"Don't worry about that. Both Marie and the kids have a mountain of presents, they really don't need anymore. Unlike you, I haven't been allowed to forget what day it is today."

He laughed at his own words. "It's amazing how even little kids seem to know that presents are the most important thing about the holidays!"

He shook his head but Lucas could hear the pride in Dan's voice. He couldn't recall exactly how old the twins were, a fact that shamed him a little. It made him realise that his life consisted of work and not much else. That thought was more painful than he had counted on, maybe if he'd made more of an effort to have a relationship with someone, he wouldn't now have to rely on his partner's generosity to avoid spending Christmas on his own. But that was stupid, really. He'd always enjoyed his own company, he'd never felt lonely before, at least not for a long time and yet, seeing Dan and Marie interact with their kids and with each other as they sat enjoying Christmas dinner, both of them working as team to look after their kids, he thought that maybe, if he managed to hang on to his job, he would try and make more of an effort to have some sort of social life. How successful that would turn out remained to be seen.

While Marie put the kids down for a nap, the men cleared up the kitchen and then went to watch the game on the huge TV hanging on the wall of the living room. The place was comfortably furnished, toys and bits of wrapping paper still littering the carpet, testimony to the fact that a family lived here. Thinking of his own sparse living space, Lucas realised with disturbing clarity that life was passing him by. He remembered the way his parents had always made a special effort for him at Christmas, decorating the house, his mother in charge of the inside, whilst he and his Dad were tasked with setting up the lights on the outside. In fact, there had been friendly competition amongst the neighbours to see who could have the best light display.

"Lucas, I won't ask you any details but, man, it must be tough for you right now."

Dan's simple statement pulled him from his thoughts and he realised, he actually wanted to talk to his friend.

"It's all kinds of fucked up!" He sighed. "But I tell you, the woman I met was sweet and kind of shy, you know? I get that this sounds stupid but I really didn't pick up any killer vibes!"

He added the last bit with a shake of his head.

"I got the impression that she was hiding something but never in my wildest dreams could I have imagined this!"

Dan nodded but didn't say anything so Lucas carried on.

"I've asked myself if it was all an act but ..." He trailed off, running a hand through his hair. "I just can't understand why she called again? By this time, she knew what I did for a living so why would she ring?"

"I don't know. Did she ever ask you about the investigation?" Dan asked.

"No, that's just it, she never mentioned it. We talked about other stuff. With hindsight, I guess it was weird that we never talked about it, but at the time, it never occurred to me. Maybe I was thinking too much about other stuff, if you know what I mean?" He grinned at Dan despite the topic.

Dan nodded. "From what I saw of the picture they did of her, I'm not surprised!" He laughed.

Lucas smiled. "Did they allow you to listen to the interview?"

He needed to know if his partner had heard everything he'd told Tom in that room. He was relieved when Dan shook his head.

"No, and to be honest, I didn't really want to so when I was told to wait, I wasn't unhappy about it."

He gave Lucas a pensive look.

"I can imagine that it must have been difficult for you. Finding out you had a personal connection to a serial killer can't have been pleasant. But I know one thing about you Lucas, you are dedicated to the job and no one can question your integrity. I mean, you couldn't make this shit up!" He grinned, slightly embarrassed.

Lucas had to laugh too. Hearing Dan's words made him feel a little better about the situation. He knew he hadn't given anything away as far as the investigation was concerned. The private part of his brief relationship with Sabrina, if it could be called that, was another matter. But he was only human and the connection he'd felt from the first moment of meeting her had been real, however fucked up this now seemed.

"Thanks, Dan. That means a lot!"

When Marie joined them a little later, the conversation turned to lighter topics, much to Lucas's relief. He was basically a private man and although he realised it had been good to talk to Dan about it, he didn't really want to say anymore. When the baby alarm went off, indicating that the twins had finished napping, he got up.

"Thank you both for your generosity. I really appreciate it."

Marie laughed and came to give him a hug.

"Don't be silly, Lucas. It's been too long since we all had a get together." She looked up at him, a concerned look in her eyes. "You'll be okay, yeah?"

He nodded with a smile. "I guess."

After saying good bye, loaded up with plastic containers filled with left overs, he got his car keys back from Dan.

"I'm sorry I won't be there tomorrow." He said and Dan nodded.

"I'm sure you'll be back before you know it!"

Dan's words were meant to be reassuring but Lucas still couldn't fathom out how his involvement with Sabrina would affect his job. He nodded and, with a final wave, walked out to his car.

He woke up the next morning with a raging hangover. Groaning, he rubbed his throbbing temples, wondering why he'd thought it was a good idea to drink half a bottle of Scotch as he'd sat in his living room, going over the same questions in his mind over and over. He gingerly got out of bed and padded into his bathroom. Swallowing two painkillers, he hoped they would make him feel better sooner rather than later. He splashed cold water on his face and then went to make some coffee. As he stood waiting for the machine to finish, he wondered how the investigation was going back in DC. Dan had been recalled over there and Lucas couldn't help but feel annoyed at being left out of the loop, even though he understood that there was no way he could continue working on the case. Several cups of coffee later, he showered and then decided that this would be an ideal time to clear out some of the garbage that had accumulated over the years, clogging up his garage and leaving him having to park on the road. Might as well use this enforced vacation for something useful! Putting on some old jeans, he switched on the garage light, surveiling the mess. Shaking his head, he started to clear one corner although he knew his heart wasn't in it when he found himself moving the same box containing old books from his Dad's place for the third time. Lucas wondered whether it was lunch time yet, at least he would have a valid excuse to stop this pointless exercise when he heard someone knock on his door. Wondering who it could be, he poked his head outside and was surprised to find a young guy standing on his porch, holding a small package.

."Are you Lucas Green?" He said after glancing down at his tablet to check the name.

"Yep, that's me." Lucas walked over to the porch.

The guy handed over the package and then held out the tablet towards Lucas.

"Sign here." He said, pointing at the screen.

Lucas picked up the little plastic pen attached to the tablet by a curly wire and scribbled his name before handing the tablet back to the guy.

"Thanks! Have a good day." With that, the guy turned and walked back to his truck, whistling as he went about his business.

Lucas stared at the package, wondering what on Earth it was and more importantly, who had sent it. The small label only stated his address with no information about the sender to be found anywhere. With a sigh, he walked back through the garage, closing the door behind himself and went through to the kitchen, putting the parcel on the table. He poured himself another cup, staring at the small parcel as if he was expecting it to blow up any minute. Shaking his head, he got out a knife and cut open the wrapping. Surprised, he found himself holding a blue and white gift box, taped closed. It had no markings of any kind on it. Picking up the knife again, he sliced through the tape and opened the lid. Inside was a neatly folded handwritten note and his heart stopped when he recognised the writing. He sat down heavily, his hands shaking slightly as he unfolded the note.

Lucas,

I know that by know, you will know who I am, or rather, what I am. I have enclosed everything you will need to close all the outstanding cases but I have added an extra part, explaining why. I suppose you think there is no reason good enough to explain why I did what I did but all I ask of you is that you at least read it and then pass judgement.

I also want to tell you that despite everything, when I was with you, I felt like a 'normal' person, not some sick killer. And please believe me when I say that what I wrote on the note after our night together was the most honest thing I have ever said.

I am sorry you got involved with me in the first place, it must put you in an extremely difficult position. I can't regret meeting you though, I only wish that I had met you years ago. If I had, then maybe things would have turned out differently. But we all make choices and mine were bad ones, I can see that now. You were the only good thing to happen to me in a very long time and for that I am truly grateful.

I hope the enclosed will help you to salvage your job, solving all seven cases will surely go a long way towards that. You're a good man, Lucas and I wish I could have been a better woman for you.

One last request. Please don't let anyone else read this note. I have written this for your eyes only, all relevant facts are in the file marked with my real name.

Sabrina

Completely stunned, Lucas read the note again. He looked in the small box and saw it contained several USB sticks. He emptied them out onto the table and as he looked closer, he saw that each one of them had been labelled with the name of one of her victims on it, as well as the date of their murder. One of them however, had only a name on it. He had to look twice at the name, written in small neat writing, his mind not understanding immediately what he was seeing. Picking it up, Lucas went into the living room and got his laptop out. He powered up the system and then plugged the stick into the port on the side. It contained only one file, titled Sabrina Heffner-O'Hare. He opened the document and started to read. Lucas didn't notice the tears that wet his cheeks as he read her story. She had written an extensive and detailed account of her life and what had driven her to do what she did. His heart broke at the thought of the distraught young girl who had fled that night. She'd endured a terrible attack and had been abandoned years before, even by her own mother. After years of neglect and subjected to mental abuse, both by the Senator and her mother, he wasn't surprised to find himself understanding her a little better. It excused in no way what she'd done but under the circumstances, he could see how she'd ended up a killer. The document ended with the killing of the Senator and her subsequent flight out of the hotel. He wondered where she was now. Was she still in DC? Somehow, he doubted it. Thinking over what he'd just read, Lucas suddenly realised something. She had given him her real name that night and he now understood why she'd been so panicked when she'd introduced herself. In a strange way, he was pleased that she'd at least given him that. He wondered why she'd done that, for all he would have known, any name would have done. Thinking about that for a bit, he thought he knew why. Sabrina had felt the same connection as he had, he was sure. To him, it was the only logical explanation for her slip up. At that moment, she'd been herself. With a sigh, he wiped his wet cheeks and then closed the file, pulling the stick from its port. Putting it with the others still scattered over his kitchen table, he carefully swept them back into the small box, not wanting to contaminate what he knew to be evidence with his prints. The note however, did not go back in the box. Even though he knew he should hand it over to forensics, Lucas just couldn't bring himself to do it. It contained nothing that would aid the investigations and he felt no hesitation at granting her wish to destroy it. He lit one of the burners on his stove and held the paper against the flame before dropping the burning paper into the sink, watching as the flames ate up her words. He switched on the tap and flushed the little bits of ash down the pipe. Glancing at the small box, he picked up his phone and dialled Dan's number.

"Hey Lucas! What's up?" Dan sounded concerned.

"Are you busy?" Lucas asked.

"For you, no. What can I do?"

"I have something here that I need you to see. Can you come over?"

Dan was silent for a moment. "Yeah, I'll be there in half an hour."

He hung up without asking any further questions and Lucas paced his living room floor until he heard Dan pull up outside. He opened the door and then went into the kitchen, pointing at the box.

"Put on some gloves, Dan. This is evidence."

His curt words made Dan look at him, his eyes curious but he did as he was told and pulled out a pair of latex gloves from his pocket. Picking up the box, he removed the lid and then looked over at Lucas, eyebrows raised in question.

"What's this?"

Lucas sighed. "It was delivered earlier. It's from Sabrina."

He pointed to the contents of the box. "Have a look at the labels."

Dan studied the small writing and then let out a curse. "Are these what I think they are?"

Lucas nodded. "There is one extra though, it's got Sabrina's name on it."

Again, he waited to see Dan's reaction.

"Fuck me! She was the Senator's daughter?"

Lucas shook his head. "Step daughter."

He paused for a moment, feeling almost protective of the contents of that file but of course, many more people would read her story and he wondered what sort of a reaction it would provoke. Would some feel for Sabrina, like he had or would they just look at her tale as an excuse to kill?

"Have you read this?" Dan now asked.

"I have, yes, so my prints will be on this stick but not the others. I haven't touched those."

Dan looked at him and nodded. "Can I read it?"

Without a word, Lucas fetched his laptop and put it on the kitchen table.

"Help yourself."

He kept his eyes on his partner as Dan started reading. The relief he felt when he saw that Dan had to swallow hard several times as he read Sabrina's account of her life was confirmation that he wasn't the only one who could see that, despite the horrendous things she'd done, Sabrina was a lost soul, damaged beyond repair by what had happened to her. When Dan finally raised his head, he looked at Lucas and silently shook his head. Neither of them knew how to put into words what they'd read.

"Not easy reading is it?" Lucas said, breaking the long silence.

"No, it isn't. Despite of what she's done, I can't help feel some sympathy for her. Her life was one hell of a screwed-up mess and that was before she started on her killing spree."

He drew a hand through his hair. "You know I have to ask you, Lucas. Do you know where she is now?"

"No, I don't but I have been wondering about that too."

"Do you think she'll carry on with the killing?"

"No! I think the Senator was the last." Lucas replied.

Dan gave him a nod, indicating his agreement. With a sigh, he pulled out the stick and put it back in the small box with the others.

"I'll get these sent over to DC. I think Tom McClean will want to handle this. You okay with that?"

"Yeah, that would be for the best."

Dan got up and made his way to the door. "I'll let you know what happens. I heard this morning that Sabrina's picture will be shown on the main news tonight. It will be interesting to see what response we get from that. I suspect it will take a while to sort through the calls, no doubt there will be plenty of nutjobs who will claim to have seen her doing God knows what!" He gave Lucas a small grin.

Lucas nodded. "Thanks, Dan."

With a wave, Dan left and Lucas closed the door, wondering how he was going to get through the next few days. He was so used to being busy with work, he felt at a loss as to what to do. Thinking about Dan saying that Sabrina's picture would be made public today, he switched on the TV but it was too early for the news to have prepared a report already. It wasn't until the six o'clock news that the whole thing went public. He sat and listened to the news caster explaining who Sabrina was and then handed over to a specialist reporter who outlined her connection with the Senator although there was no mention of the fact that at one point, she'd been his step daughter. Instead, the report focused on her job at the Senator's office and Lucas wondered why the family link hadn't been mentioned. His phone rang and he saw a Washington number come up on the screen.

"Green." As he suspected, it was Tom McClean.

"Lucas, it's Tom. Dan sent over the evidence and we've started going through it. I have several of my team looking at the individual cases but I have read the file on the other one."

There was a moment's silence. When Lucas didn't say anything, Tom continued.

"Now I know that Dan has asked you this already but do you know where she might be?"

"No, like I told Dan, I don't."

"She's not contacted you at all, other than sending you the package?"

"No." Lucas said curtly, getting annoyed at having his statement questioned. "If she did, I would tell you, believe me!"

"Okay, make sure that you do. We'll see what happens with the picture. The Senator's secretary made a positive identification, so we are sure that Sabrina and Katie Palmer are one and the same. She was distraught when she realised she'd actually taking a liking to Katie." Tom said.

"It would appear that she's a good actress."

He didn't say anything else but Lucas got the distinct impression his comment was meant as some sort of consolation to Lucas, implying that he'd not been the only one to be fooled by Sabrina.

"Let's hope we get lucky and find her before she kills again."

"She won't!" Lucas said harshly.

"How do you know that, Agent Green."

Good question, Lucas thought. How could he explain that he was sure that she would not kill again, he had no facts to back up his conviction.

"Let's say I have a gut feeling. I haven't anything else to give you Tom. But I am sure she's done."

"Okay, I'll be in touch."

With that, he hung up. Lucas wasn't sure if Tom had believed him but he didn't care. They had all the evidence they needed to close the files on seven murders, catching the killer on the loose was an entirely different story though. And if she was arrested? What would he do? Would he go and see her, ask for answers to the many questions her confession had raised? Lucas didn't know. Although it was little early in the evening, he pulled a beer from the fridge. Maybe he would order some dinner although he had no appetite. Rummaging through the drawer where he kept his take-out leaflets, he didn't know what he wanted so he would have a look at what might sound appealing. His gaze fell on a small piece of paper with a number written on it. He pulled it out and stood staring at it for some time. Would the phone still be switched on? He remembered the burner phone that had been used for the Saunders case. It would be a reasonable assumption that Sabrina would have gotten rid of this one too. But what if she hadn't? Debating whether to try and call her, Lucas fought against his wish to talk to her. He should send the number to Tom and his team. If she still had it on her, it would be a way of tracing her whereabouts. Could he do it? Be responsible for her apprehension, knowing that she would die in prison? Pacing his kitchen, he wrangled with his conscience. He felt empty when he finally picked up the phone and punched in the number, waiting for the person on the other end to answer.

Chapter 32

Sabrina thought it ironic that she was right back in the same place she'd fled only a few days ago. Her need to run had been strong but she'd realised that there was really no other place she could go. It didn't matter where she went, her past would always be there and she could no longer pretend to be able to start over somewhere else. So, she'd come back, focused on the one place she hoped would bring her some peace. Before leaving the airport, she stopped at a Flower shop and bought a large bouquet of flowers and then hailed a cab. When she told the driver where she wanted to go, he just nodded, obviously not in the least bit wondering about her destination. They hit the rush hour traffic and by the time they arrived, night had fallen.

"You sure about going in there?" The driver asked.

"Yes, thank you."

"Want me to wait for you?" This time, his voice showed concern but she shook her head.

"That won't be necessary, I'm having a friend pick me up in a little while but thank you."

The driver shrugged his shoulders and Sabrina handed over the fare before getting out the cab, watching as the red tail lights disappeared into the night. With a sigh, she made her way to the gates of the cemetery. She hadn't been here since the day of the funeral but she'd always sent flowers on her mother's birthday and on the anniversary of her death. Despite having been at the grave side only the one time, she found her way through the numerous rows of stones without any problems. Her mother's grave had no decoration other than the head stone itself, the last lot of flowers she'd sent had long since faded and had been removed. Carefully, she knelt down and placed the bunch of flowers on the grave, arranging them so they leaned against the pale marble, partially covering up the gold lettering. The nearest street light cast a shadow but Sabrina wasn't scared. Instead, she finally felt a sense of peace, being near her Mama. She sat for a long time, not feeling the cold seeping into her bones as she sat on the grass. Starting from at the day of the funeral, she told her mother what she'd done during the intervening years, tears finally flowing. Sabrina didn't bother to wipe her eyes, she just continued, her voice quiet but steady.

The vibration of her phone ringing in her bag brought her monologue to a halt. She pulled it out and looked at the screen. Of course, she knew who was calling and she thought she knew what that meant for her. With a weary sigh, she answered.

"Hello?"

"Sabrina?" Lucas sounded hesitant.

"Yes."

She waited for him to speak, wanting very badly for him to tell her that everything was going to be okay but that was delusional. She did know why he'd called and her heart hurt at the thought of yet another betrayal. But she understood, had known that he would do his duty, he'd sworn an oath to protect the public from people like her.

"Where are you?" His voice was gentle and Sabrina felt fresh tears falling.

"I'm home." She didn't care if he heard that she was crying, years of unspent tears could no longer be denied.

"Please tell me where you are, Sabrina. If I can, I'll come to you."

"I know what you're doing, Lucas and it's okay, really. How much longer before they trace the call?"

Her words held no accusation, instead there was only relief. His silence told her everything she needed to know.

"I'm glad you called, Lucas. I wasn't sure whether you would, given the situation." She swallowed a sob.

"I don't know if anyone is listening to this conversation but I want to tell you that I am so glad I met you. You were the only person in a very long time who made me feel special and for that I am grateful. But I am also sorry you got mixed up in my life, I just hope that one day, you'll be able to forgive me."

"There is nothing to forgive, Sabrina. After reading your file, I understand a little better and I am just sorry that you had no one to turn to for help."

His voice was thick, almost as if he too was on the verge of tears.

"Thank you, Lucas, that means a lot. But I chose to do what I did, no excuses and I've made peace with that." She paused for a moment.

"Can I ask you one last favour?"

"Anything!" Lucas replied instantly.

"Please stay in Baltimore. Don't come here and if you can avoid it, don't try and see me again. I would prefer it if you could remember me the way I was the last time we were together."

For a long moment, Sabrina didn't think he would reply.

"Okay." His voice was calm and steady. "I'm off the case so I don't need to be involved, other than as a potential witness."

And there it was! She'd known but still, it hurt. Time to end the call, she guessed it wouldn't be long before the cemetery would be crawling with law enforcement.

"You take care now, Lucas."

She whispered and then hung up, switching the phone off altogether. She lent back against her mother's headstone and waited for what seemed like a long time. In the quiet night and with her senses on high alert, she would be able to hear approaching footfall, even if the people coming for her were stealthy. She smiled as she pulled the brown envelope from her bag, shaking the small brown bottle into her hand. She unscrewed the lid and sat looking at the innocent looking capsule in the palm of her hand, gently wrapping her fingers around it. She was ready.

Chapter 33

"McClean." Tom's voice was cool but Lucas could hear the stress in the inflection of the words.

"Tom, it's Lucas."

"What can I do for you, Agent Green?"

Lucas told him about the phone number.

"I don't know if it's still operational but I guess, your guys can find out." He hoped his tone gave nothing away of the turmoil he felt. He'd been torn, but in the end, he knew there was only one thing he could do.

"Leave it with me." Tom said. "Thank you, Lucas. I can imagine that wasn't an easy decision to make but you did the right thing."

"Yeah, I know!" Lucas didn't know what else to say.

"I'll keep you informed." Tom said and then hung up.

All he could do now was wait. He fought the urge to try the number, knowing that the team in DC would try and locate Sabrina, if the phone was switched on. It was only a short while later that he got a call back from Tom McClean.

"Here's the situation. The phone is switched on but because there are so many towers here in DC, it would take us a long time to pinpoint her exact location. "Tom said without any preamble.

"I want you to call her and keep her on the phone until we get an exact location. Three minutes should do it. You okay with that?"

Lucas knew it wasn't really a question, he had little choice. He was an FBI Agent, it was his job to bring criminals to justice and, whether he liked it or not, that's what Sabrina was.

"Sure! Want me to call right away?"

His tone was flat. He couldn't and wouldn't think about the repercussions for Sabrina, he had a job to do and that was that.

"Yeah, we're set up this end. We'll be monitoring the call, if she answers." Tom said, letting him know without saying it out loud that whatever was going to be said during the next few minutes would be recorded and used as evidence.

With a sigh, he hung up and then dialled Sabrina.

"Hello?"

Her voice was quiet but Lucas could hear that she'd been crying. He felt a pang in his chest but, taking a deep breath, he spoke.

"Sabrina?"

It was evident from the start that she knew what was happening and yet, there was no recrimination in her voice, just bone deep sadness. He panicked when she whispered her goodbye and hung up, cursing as he threw down his phone. Almost immediately, it rang again.

"Good work, Lucas. We've got her location. We've got a team going out as we speak." Tom said.

"Where is she?" Lucas felt sick but he needed to know.

"At the cemetery where her mother is buried. We should have it all cleared up within an hour. I'll call you later with an update."

"No! I'm coming over. Let me be the one to bring her in."

There was a short pause and Lucas waited with baited breath. He knew he needed to be there, regardless of what he'd promised to Sabrina earlier.

"Not sure that's possible, Lucas." Tom said but Lucas ploughed on.

"You make it possible SAC McClean! Thanks to me, you've got all you need to convict her. I want to see this through to the end. Give me an hour and I'll be there."

He wasn't above pointing out the obvious if it meant he could do this his way.

After what seemed an eternity, Tom spoke.

"An hour, that's all, Agent Green. I warn you though, if she moves, we're going in, whether you're here or not."

Tom gave him the location details and hung up without another word.

Breaking all kinds of speed limits on the way to DC, Lucas kept glancing at his watch, seeing the minutes trickle away. He had only a few minutes to spare when he pulled up at the imposing gates of the cemetery. The stillness of the cemetery should have been eerie, but instead, Lucas found the surrounding darkness comforting, the occasional street light illuminating just enough of the path leading deeper into the cemetery. He passed many old tombs, the weathered stones a poignant reminder of how fleeting life was. When he finally spotted Sabrina, he stepped off the pathway and stood in the shadows for a moment. Her head bent, she seemed to be talking to someone although he knew they were alone, for now. When she spoke, he nearly jumped out of his skin.

"You aren't supposed to be here, Lucas."

Her voice was soft but tinged with sadness. Her words, though spoken quietly carried clearly in the still night.

He stepped back onto the path. How had she known it was him?

"You have to know that I had to come, Sabrina." He replied and took a few steps towards her, trying not to spook her.

She turned at his approach, looking at him with a sad little smile on her beautiful face that held traces of her earlier tears.

"Why?"

Her question reminded him of their very first meeting and his heart contracted.

"I think you know why, Sabrina. From the very first time we met, we had a connection, you and I."

He took another couple of steps towards her.

"Yes." She said, nodding. "I'm sorry."

"What are you sorry about, Sabrina?"

The sombre light of the street lamp a little further along the path from where she sat cast shadows over her face. He was close enough to see her features clearly although she looked different somehow. He realised that she'd changed the colour of her hair. It was an odd thing to notice given the situation but Lucas knew it was more than that. Sabrina knew what was waiting for her, she knew that she would end her days in prison. And yet, he didn't see any agitation or fear on her face. She looked calm, sitting there with her arms around her knees as if she did this sort of thing every day.

"I should never have accepted your offer of a drink that night in the bar." Her words sent a pang through his chest.

"Are you sorry we ever got together?" Lucas asked.

"No! Not that, not ever. But if I had walked away like I should have, then all of this would be a lot simpler for you now, wouldn't it?"

Lucas thought about that. "Maybe so but you didn't, did you? Walk away and despite everything, I am not sorry that you didn't."

"Like I said, I'm sorry." Sabrina shook her head sadly.

"Even though I meant every word when I wrote you that note, I still regret not having walked away, if only to spare you."

Lucas went to move towards her but she put a hand up in warning.

"Please don't come any closer!"

Her voice was still low but he could hear the steel in it, stopping him in his tracks. It only just occurred to him that he'd left his gun at home, he'd come away in such a rush, he'd never even thought to bring it.

"Don't worry, I won't hurt you." Sabrina said and once again, Lucas was struck by her uncanny ability to read him.

"I never thought you would." He said, letting her hear the sincerity of his words.

"Are the others here yet?" Her gaze turned back to the grave.

"I'm not sure but I guess they're not too far. I was given an hour to come and see you."

His words made her clasp her knees a little tighter, the sadness radiating from her almost palpable.

"I really wish you hadn't come here, Lucas because you have to know how much harder this makes it for me."

He saw a tear sliding down her cheek and had to fight the urge to rush to her, to take her in his arms and tell her that all would be okay. He couldn't do that though, because they both knew that nothing was ever going to be okay again. Not for either of them. Instead, he watched her sitting there, her hands clasped together. Picking up a bottle of water resting against her bag beside her, Sabrina sighed and straightened her shoulders, pushing a weary hand through her hair. Lucas watched as the light reflected on the blonde strands, so different to the dark hair the last time he'd seen her. With her head back, she took several sips and then dropped the bottle before returning back to her previous pose, fingers once again interlaced over her knees.

"Although I am glad in a way, at least I'm not alone." She took a deep breath as if she was struggling to get her words out.

"You've been alone for a long time."

His simple statement hung in the still night air between them.

"I have, but that was mostly my own choice. At least, after …"

She didn't finish her sentence but Lucas knew what she was referring to.

"I am sorry that you had no one to lean on, Sabrina." Lucas said softly but she didn't reply.

Lucas waited, his eyes focused on her and saw that she was shaking, a low moan escaping from her parted lips. Disregarding her warning not to get any closer, he closed the distance between them. Her head was bent, a hand on her stomach, fingers flexing as if she was in pain.

"Sabrina?"

He felt a sense of rising panic and was shocked to the core when she finally looked up. For the first time, he saw the real Sabrina, her beautiful blue eyes full of tears, her lovely face contorted with pain. Alarmed, Lucas crouched down next to her. He reached out and touched her face, shocked at how cold she was. Another low moan escaped her lips as little droplets of sweat appeared on her smooth forehead. With a curse, he sat down next to her, picking her up and trying to warm her with his own body heat. She felt small and fragile in his arms, her body shaking and her breathing becoming more and more laboured. Holding her this close with her head resting against his chest, he finally realised what was happening.

"Oh Sabrina!"

He was distraught, knowing that there was nothing he could do to save her. So, he just held her tighter, hoping she would feel less alone.

"I could have loved you, Lucas."

Her voice was barely a whisper but the words shredded his heart. His tears fell into her blonde hair as he felt her take her final breath.

"I could have loved you too." He whispered, taking deep breaths in an attempt to regain his equilibrium. The woman in his arms was finally at peace but Lucas wasn't sure if he ever would.

He wasn't sure how long it was before he heard footsteps approach and as he looked up, he saw Tom McClean standing there, gun in hand.

"Step away, Lucas." Tom held his gaze for a moment. "We'll take it from here."

Lucas nodded, part of him unwilling to let her go, yet he knew that he had to comply. Just because she'd taken her own live didn't mean that the wheels that had been set in motion so many years ago would now stop turning. With a resigned sigh, he carefully laid Sabrina on the ground and then stood up and moved away without a backward glance.

Other people suddenly crowded the space around the grave, lights were being set up, the scene had to be secured and evidence gathered. Lucas had done this himself countless times but he just could not bring himself to hang around so he carried on walking, ignoring Tom's calls to stay put. More people passed him on his way back to the car but he ignored them all.

Walking through the gates, he was astonished to find Dan standing beside his car.

"What are you doing here?" He asked, his voice hollow.

"Tom called me." Dan said simply and opened the passenger door for him. "Come on, I'll take you home."

Lucas did as he was told, neither of them speaking the entire way back to Baltimore, Lucas too shocked by what had happened and Dan sensitive enough to realise that. Pulling up outside his house, Lucas swallowed in an attempt to speak.

"Thanks, Dan."

He didn't say anything else and when Dan nodded wordlessly, he opened the car door and got out, making his way slowly to his front door. Half a bottle of Scotch later, he passed out on his sofa, sinking gratefully into oblivion.

Chapter 34

The day following Sabrina's death was a complete nightmare, starting with Lucas waking up to the hangover from hell. Despite numerous coffees and several painkillers, his mind remained foggy, the turmoil from events of the previous night still swirling around. He'd been given orders to report back to the DC office and Dan was waiting for him outside by eight o'clock. Despite his best efforts, Lucas knew he looked like shit and judging by Dan's expression, he wasn't wrong.

"You sleep at all?" Dan asked with a frown.

Lucas shrugged, wishing his head would stop hurting.

"Not much. I guess it didn't help that I got drunk on half a bottle of Scotch. Again!"

Dan couldn't help the small smile as he looked at his partner.

"Yeah, understandable as it is, perhaps not the best idea you ever had, huh?"

Lucas groaned.

"Just drive, will you?" He sighed and then apologised.

"I'm sorry. None of this is your fault. Thanks for picking me up, I'm pretty sure I'm still over the limit." Despite his roiling stomach and pounding head, he had to smile as Dan grinned at him and then pulled away from the curb.

They didn't speak much for the rest of the journey, but Lucas felt a little better by the time they arrived at the FBI headquarters. Once again, Tom McClean was waiting for them.

"Morning." Tom gave Lucas the once over but didn't make any comments about his obviously hungover state.

"Agent Green, you're with me. Agent Mortimer, you head up to the main office and go find Jack Simmons. I've put together a team of people to work though the files. Your help will be welcome."

Dan nodded and, with a final look at Lucas, made his way to the bank of elevators.

"Follow me." Tom said to Lucas and turned down a side corridor, Lucas trailing behind silently.

A short while later, he found himself in an interview room once again, an exact copy of the previous one. Taking a seat, he watched as Tom placed a folder on the table and then gave him a sharp look.

"You want a coffee?"

"Thanks, that would be good."

"Don't make a habit of this, Agent Green." Tom's voice held a small trace of sympathy.

"What do you mean? Getting drunk, associate with serial killers, what?"

Lucas knew he was being a dick but really, there was nothing Tom could hold against him that he hadn't already thought of. Of course, he knew that drinking himself into a stupor wasn't a clever thing to do. As for the other, he couldn't undo the last few months and, despite everything, even if he could, he wouldn't. He couldn't regret having known Sabrina but at the same time, he knew he had to let her go. He just wasn't entirely sure at this moment in time how he was going to do that.

"Both!" Tom said, clearly not amused by his attitude. Lucas held up a hand.

"Sorry, that was unprofessional." He let out a weary sigh. "Let's just get on with this, okay?"

Tom looked at him for a moment and then nodded.

"Let's start with you ignoring my orders to stay put last night. I'm sure I don't need to tell you that, under normal circumstances, you'd be in all sorts of trouble right now."

He raised a brow, but Lucas just nodded. What could he possibly say?

"Given what had happened, I'm prepared to let that go. I understand that last night was difficult." He opened the folder and studied the papers in it for a moment.

"We've had the tox report back from the lab. Sabrina took a massive overdose of Barbiturates, mixed with some other lethal poisons, arsenic and a few others. She was efficient to the end."

Lucas recoiled at his words. The truth of Tom's words was undeniable, yet he couldn't help but be amazed at how Sabrina had indeed thought to cover every eventuality. He couldn't even begin to understand how her mind had worked. Not only because of what she'd been capable of but also to think so far ahead as to have a suicide pill at the ready, just in case.

Not waiting for a reply, Tom continued.

"I have read the file about her life. You were right about many things, Lucas. How much of it did she tell you about?"

"None of it. The only thing I knew before reading her account was that she had no family."

Tom looked at him questioningly. "I find that hard to believe. I mean, you took the woman out, what did you talk about?"

Lucas gave him a sharp look.

"I already told you what was said during my last interview. She spoke about her job search, about her work at the dog shelters, but nothing too personal."

He was pissed that he had to repeat himself. What was McClean getting at with this line of questioning? As soon as he'd asked himself that question, he understood. Anger fired his blood.

"Now wait just a minute! Do you really think I was in on this? That she told me she was going after the Senator and I didn't do anything to stop her?"

He nearly shouted the last bit, seriously annoyed now. Before Tom could reply, he continued.

"Can I just remind you, Special Agent in Charge McClean that it was me who sent you the files. I was the one to give you the number to locate her so whatever it is you're implying here is bullshit!"

"I am fully aware of that, Agent Green!" Tom replied coolly. "But you have to see things from my perspective. You knew the killer intimately, she sent you the details of all her murders and even gave you her number so you could keep in contact. So, I am asking myself, how is it that she did all that and yet, you claim to have known nothing of her other life as a serial killer."

The look he gave Lucas left no doubt that Tom wasn't buying his version of events.

"I have asked myself that countless times." Lucas sighed and rubbed his temple.

"The only thing I can tell you is that when she was with me, Sabrina was not acting in any way suspicious. Perhaps you could say that she came across as someone with issues, but that was more to do with her feeling inadequate when it came to dating. I always thought that something must have happened in her past that made her wary of men but never, and I mean never did it cross my mind to suspect her of the X murders!" He shrugged.

"Maybe that makes me a bad agent, not being able to see through her façade, but what it doesn't do is make me in any way shape or form, guilty by association."

Tom gave him a pensive look.

"Perhaps, but then you need to explain your behaviour from last night. You approached a known serial killer unarmed and without fear. How did you know she wouldn't attack you? You'd betrayed her and, given the state of her mind, it would seem, that this was reason enough to kill you too."

Lucas shook his head. "I didn't know. The thought had crossed my mind when I spoke to her but after reading her file, I kind of knew she was done killing. If you think about it, the last ten years of her life were spent running from the Senator, figuratively speaking. During all those years, she made no attempt to contact him. It wasn't until she saw that he was getting married again that she decided to go after him. Because she saw an exact copy of her fate waiting for the little girl whose mother was marrying that monster. I'm no psychologist but it stands to reason that this was the trigger and with it, the start of the end. Once the Senator was dead, she had no purpose left, at least in her mind."

Lucas lent back in his chair and watched the man across from him, waiting for what came next. Tom's next words took him by surprise.

"You're a very good agent, Lucas. That is obvious from the reasoning behind your thoughts. However, you wouldn't be the first man to have his head turned by a pretty face."

He held up a hand as Lucas opened his mouth to respond to his words.

"I'm not saying that this is what happened! Like you said, you played the biggest part in stopping her. But I want to know why you went unarmed to meet with a known serial killer? You knew by then that she'd been meticulous in everything she did. I have never seen such dedication to making sure everything, and I mean everything went as she'd planned. If I had been in your position, I would have been armed to the teeth. So, why?" Tom leaned back, looking at Lucas.

"I've already told you!" Lucas said with a sigh. "It never occurred to me, that it could potentially be dangerous for me. When you told me you'd found her, all I was thinking about was that I needed to be there. You got to understand, that with our history, and despite knowing what she was, I never once felt threatened whilst I was in her company."

"Okay." Tom shuffled through the papers in the file. Surprised by his easy acquiescence, Lucas wondered what McClean was coming up with next.

"We found a parking pass in Sabrina's purse from Orlando airport."

"So that's where she went!" Lucas interrupted.

What had she been doing down there? Could it be possible that she was preparing for her next victim? He shook his head. That didn't make any sense, she only stayed a couple of days and then came back to DC. He couldn't even begin to understand the state of her mind but one thing he knew, she'd been suffering. He'd seen it in her eyes last night, all the pain she'd endured, some caused by the hand of others but mostly, he thought, at the realisation of what she'd let herself become.

"I've sent a team down to check out her car. We've found nothing else of any importance in the bag she had with her, so it stands to reason, that she left most of her luggage in the car. I'm hoping we can get our hands on that suit of hers. From the description she left, our forensics team will have field day with it."

Tom's words made Lucas angry.

"You need more evidence? Is it not enough that she's given detailed accounts of every murder?"

Tom gave him a cool look. "If you weren't so closely linked to her, maybe you too could understand my way of thinking. Yes, we do have enough evidence, not that it matters now since there won't be a trial, but you seem to fail to understand the significance of finding out as much as we can about how she operated, Agent Green. Anything we can learn from how she managed to evade the law for seven years will be considered helpful, at least in my book!"

Lucas leaned back in his chair, grudgingly having to admit that McClean was right. He really was too close to see the important, bigger picture.

"Of course, you're right. Apologies."

He rubbed his still throbbing temple. A nod of acceptance was all he got from the man sitting opposite him.

"I think we're done here for now." Tom stood, picking up his paperwork.

"Go home, Agent Green. We'll take care of the rest of the investigation."

Lucas stood up, unwilling to be excluded. He needed to help finalise everything because he knew that if he didn't, he'd always be tied to Sabrina in some way.

"I want to help." He sighed, dragging a hand over his face. "No, scrap that! I need to help."

McClean looked at him for a long moment, his cool gaze assessing.

"You're off the case, Green."

"I know that but as you said, there will be no trial, so I can't see how my being involved in closing down the files could be a problem."

Lucas could tell by the look on the other man's face that he wasn't convinced.

"Look, I'll spell it out for you. I really need to see this through, otherwise …"

Lucas couldn't and wouldn't go any further. He felt foolish enough but explaining to Tom that unless he managed to draw a line under events, he feared he'd never get over Sabrina. And that wasn't something he wanted to do.

"Go and find your partner, Agent Green."

With a curt nod, Tom left the office, but Lucas had seen enough in his parting gaze to realise that McClean had understood. Relieved, he followed him out of the interrogation room and went to find Dan.

Chapter 35

The immediate aftermath had created a media storm, as was to be expected. The headlines were sometimes hard to bear. Just like most of his fellow agents, the press only saw the serial killer. The woman behind that persona was totally ignored. Nobody thought to dig a little deeper, no one could see what he had seen. Sabrina hadn't been born a psychopath but had, to some extent at least, been a victim of circumstances. But perhaps that was just as well. Lucas had no desire to talk about his personal involvement with Sabrina. Although the Bureau managed to keep that bit out of the press, there were several times Lucas and Dan had been approached by some eager journalist, wanting the inside story of the X Murderer. They ever commented, always referring them to the press office at HQ.

Neither the public nor the press knew that on the day of Sabrina's funeral, an old couple had stood beside him at the grave side, tears for the little girl they had once known and loved, running freely. Their contact details had been found among some papers they'd recovered from Sabrina's possessions, left behind in the car at the airport in Orlando. It turned out that she'd paid off the mortgage on their small cottage anonymously, thus ensuring a peaceful and comfortable retirement for Joshua and Annie, people who had meant so much to her. When Lucas had volunteered to go and interview them as part of the investigation, he'd found them heart broken.

Pulling up in front of the small house, Lucas didn't quite know what to expect. He'd briefly spoken to Joshua Mayer on the phone, telling him that he needed to speak to them regarding Sabrina, without going into any further details. The old man had sounded shocked but hadn't made any comment. Lucas knocked on the front door, noting that it and the whole house in general were very well maintained. The man opening the door stood tall, his long grey hair gathered in the nape of his neck in a ponytail.

"Mr. Mayer? I'm FBI Agent Lucas Green. We spoke on the phone?"

Lucas extended a hand and held out his badge. The man studied it carefully before nodding.

"We did. Come in."

He turned without another word and Lucas followed, not entirely sure of his welcome. They walked down a small hall and into a sunny kitchen, where an elderly woman stood at the sink, drying dishes. At their entrance, she turned and glanced briefly at her husband before holding out her hand in welcome.

"You must be the agent who called?" She gave him a warm smile as she shook his hand. "Please, have a seat. Would you like a coffee?"

"Thank you, Ma'am. I'm Lucas Green."

Lucas pulled out one of the chairs and sat down at the kitchen table, glancing around the room. It was small but cosy, the walls painted in a light yellow giving the room a warm and welcoming appearance. An old-fashioned sideboard covered nearly one entire wall, blue and white porcelain plates and cups neatly stacked on its shelves. His gaze landed on Joshua, who stood and watched him with an alertness that surprised Lucas. He hadn't exactly expected a warm welcome, but he didn't know what to make of the man. He had an uncomfortable feeling that he was being assessed and wondered whether the final conclusion would be favourable.

"There you are." Annie placed cups and saucers on the table along with a plate of cookies, sugar and milk. "I don't know how you take your coffee, Agent Green."

She gave him a smile, pointing to the table. "Just help yourself."

"Thank you, that's very kind."

With a nod to her husband, she pulled out a chair facing Lucas and pointed to the one next to her. Her husband sat beside her, still not speaking and Lucas figured he would have to start the conversation.

"Thank you both for agreeing to speak with me. I understand that you had no contact with Sabrina since her mother sold the house and married the Senator?"

Annie nodded but it was Joshua who spoke.

"That's correct. We took our retirement when Serena, Sabrina's mother, sold up."

His tone was curt, but Lucas thought he could hear a trace of regret in Joshua's voice.

"Broke our hearts, that did!" Annie said, her eyes sad. "We loved Sabrina like she was our granddaughter and it was hard to see how unhappy she was at having to leave her childhood home. Worse still, she had to let go of Daisy, her pony."

Annie's voice broke at the memories and she pulled out a handkerchief, wiping away her tears. Instinctively, Joshua put an arm around his wife's shoulder, the look in his eyes bleak as he tried to console her. He directed his gaze towards Lucas.

"She wrote to us for quite a while, you know. After the move, we kept in touch for a couple of years but then the letters stopped coming and we never got a reply to any of the ones we sent." He lowered his gaze, sighing. "Maybe she never got them or maybe she just forgot about us."

"No! Sabrina wouldn't have forgotten about us!" Despite the tears, Annie sounded vehement.

"You're right, Mrs. Mayer. Sabrina didn't forget you." Lucas gave her a smile.

"Did you not know that it was Sabrina who paid off your mortgage?"

The couple looked at him in shocked surprise. "That was Sabrina?"

Lucas nodded, curious to find out more.

"We found documents confirming it. Who did you think paid the loan?"

Joshua and Annie exchanged a look.

"We were told that the money had come from some distant relative we never knew. With hindsight, we should have checked it out, but we didn't." Joshua shook his head.

Lucas was amazed at how Sabrina had found a way to make sure the couple were taken care of without realising who their benefactor was.

"Why would she not have told us that the money came from her?" Joshua Mayer looked at him, clearly confused by Sabrina's subterfuge.

"I'm not sure but if I had to hazard a guess, I'd say because she'd already started killing by this point." Lucas regretted his choice of words immediately.

"Oh my God!" Annie cried, fresh tears wetting her cheeks while her husband sat back in stunned silence.

"I'm sorry!" Lucas frantically searched for the right words. "I know this hard for you, both of you but we cannot forget the reality of what she did. That may sound harsh but it's something you will have to come to terms with."

He paused, giving Annie some time to compose herself again.

"I understand that there was another side to Sabrina. A kind and caring side which many people don't or won't wish to see. She used to volunteer at various dog shelters for many years."

Annie looked at him, despite the tears, a sad smile appeared.

"Sabrina loved dogs. I'm not surprised by that."

Nodding, Lucas forced himself to refocus.

"Did you attend Serena's funeral?"

"No, we didn't know about it until we read it in the papers." Annie shook her head. "Of course, had we known, we would have been there for Sabrina. Maybe we could have helped in some way."

Fresh tears filled her eyes as she turned to her husband. "Oh Josh! The poor girl, left alone with that man ..."

She couldn't finish her sentence as sobs shook her. Lucas watched as her husband tried to calm her, the truth of her words hitting him hard. Who knew what would have happened had they been there the day of the funeral. Shaking his head, he refused to lay any blame at their feet. What was done was done, no point in speculating. He'd done enough of that already!

"Don't do that to yourself, Mrs. Mayer. There is no point in asking yourself, what if! God knows I've done it countless times!"

Both raised their heads at his outburst. "What do you mean, Agent Green?"

Lucas sighed, feeling uncomfortable but he knew, he would have to tell them.

"There's something you need to know. But before I tell you, I would appreciate your agreement that none of what you're about to hear gets out."

Wordlessly, both nodded. Taking a deep breath, Lucas told them about the chance encounter in the hotel bar and his involvement with Sabrina.

"So, you see, I understand that you might feel you could have somehow prevented what happened to Sabrina but none of us can change the past. We do what we think is best at the time and then, we must live with the consequences. I know I have to, being the one who helped find her. It was me who pulled the final strands together. Thanks to my involvement, Sabrina is no longer here. I've asked myself many times what would have happened if I hadn't made that call, the one that traced her, but you know what? I'm convinced that one way or another, she would have ended up either in prison or dead." His words echoed in the silent kitchen.

"I'm so glad she wasn't on her own at the end. Thank you, Lucas." Annie reached out and placed a hand over his.

A short while later, he wrapped up the conversation. Annie and Joshua Mayer couldn't add any further details to the investigation and he didn't want to intrude any longer. He suspected that it would be a long time before either of them managed to come to terms with what had happened.

As he stood, shaking hands with them, Annie focused her gaze on his.

"Will you let us know when and where the funeral will take place?"

Lucas nodded. It would be the least he could do.

Epilogue

Lucas stood in the weak winter sunshine, staring down at the gold lettering on the headstone, glittering as the sun's rays caressed the words etched into the pale grey marble.

Two months after that fatal night, the investigation into the X murders was officially closed. Lucas had read every file that Sabrina had compiled. Some of the contents were horrific and he found it extremely hard to reconcile the cold-blooded killer with the woman he'd shared a night with. It was as if there had been two people involved in all of this. Lucas had spoken about it to one of the psychologists attached to the Bureau after his superiors had insisted he attended at least one session. He hadn't been keen, he didn't think talking about it all to a complete stranger was going to make a difference. He'd been wrong about that.

"You have to understand, Lucas, that this is not uncommon. Serial killers often have two or even more personas. This is usually an attempt to avoid having to deal with what they're doing. In Sabrina's case, I'm not convinced that she had a split personality, but she would have needed to find a way to deal with her emotions. Separating the two in her mind, she could function, at least at some level, as a relatively normal person."

Lucas nodded. It made sense, particularly when he thought back at how animatedly Sabrina had talked about her work at the shelters.

"If you look at the last few weeks of her life, you can clearly see when the deterioration of her mind began." The psychologist, a man named Paul Cramer, was clearly very interested in Sabrina's case and had studied it in detail. *"When she saw the pictures of the Senator, it triggered the start of a descent, a downward spiral from which there would be no escape. I think it is also significant that, at the end, she'd gone back to being herself, changing her appearance to what she looked like before the attack. You may think that is a little detail, but I do believe*

that she needed to become herself again, at the end. She'd lived with being several different people for many years and I do believe that she lost a big part of her original self in the process. So, when she knew that she'd come to the end of the line, she needed to transform back to her own self in order to hang on to what little was left of her sanity."

Lucas felt a pang at the thought of Sabrina in such turmoil. He understood what the man opposite him was telling him, but he still felt that if only someone had been there for Sabrina, she could have overcome her attack. Shaking his head, he willed himself off that train of thought. It served no purpose to think of all the what ifs?

"By going to her mother's grave, Sabrina felt she'd come home. I seem to recall that this was what she said to you when you asked her where she was." Paul continued, looking at Lucas for confirmation.

"Yes, she did. At the time, I didn't understand what she meant by that but now, it makes sense."

"Indeed." Paul gave him a reassuring smile. "In her mind, being by her mother's side gave her a feeling of not being alone anymore." He paused for a moment, a sad look on his face. "You know, Lucas, despite all the horrific things she's done, I can't help but feel sympathy for her. The sequence of events that lead to her turning into a serial killer is really quite horrendous. It comes as no surprise that, left to her own devices and with no one to support her, she turned out this way."

Lucas was stunned at hearing that. It was the first time someone had put into words how he felt about Sabrina. It brought some sense of peace that he wasn't alone in thinking that Sabrina hadn't been all bad. He gave Paul a grateful smile.

"I'm glad to hear you say that. I was beginning to think that there was something wrong with me!" He paused, feeling a little embarrassed. Paul nodded encouragingly.

"Most of the other agents I've been working with seem to see her only as a killer. Maybe I would if I hadn't known that other side to her." He sighed. *"Of course, what she did was horrendous, but I cannot help feeling a sense of loss at what could have been."*

"Most of us have several sides to our psyche, so what you're feeling is not surprising. The time you spent with her was a moment out of time where she could feel like any other person, at least to some extent." Paul's voice was gentle. *"I think you shouldn't feel bad about this, Lucas. In fact, I would go so far as to say that perhaps, you gave her something she had never had and made her feel cherished, even if it was only for a very short time."* He smiled before carrying on. *"We can't always help who we develop feelings for, but you really don't need to feel ashamed or bad about that, Lucas. It says a lot about you as a man that you can separate the two."*

Memories of that night crowded him but over the past twelve months, they had lost their power to stir more than a feeling of sadness in him. Thinking back to what had happened was no longer painful although he didn't often allow himself to recall those hours. Today he let go of his self-restraint and let his mind go where it wanted. Recalling the last time he'd stood here, the day of Sabrina's funeral, he wondered how Annie and Joshua Mayer were doing. He hadn't heard from them since and maybe, that was for the best. He'd come to terms with events and had managed to return to some sort of normality. He hoped that they had too, but he guessed that, just like him, they would always remember Sabrina. Not just the serial killer but the person behind it all. In their minds, she would forever be the sunny happy child they had known and loved. As for Lucas himself, he would always remember the night they had spent together. Moving on and getting on with life didn't mean that she'd be forgotten. The one thing he had taken from all of this was that he needed to start living again. With a sigh, he carefully laid the bunch of flowers he'd brought with him on the grave, touching the head stone one last time.

"Bye Sabrina." With a final glance, he turned and made his way back to the car. He smiled as he approached the woman standing by the car, waiting for him. She placed a hand on his arm, her gaze warm.

"Okay, honey?" Her soft words, filled with concern, made him realise that he was.

The End

Printed in Poland
by Amazon Fulfillment
Poland Sp. z o.o., Wrocław